"Joe..."

Lissa murmured, gazing into his turbulent eyes.

"What is it?" Joe asked gently.

"I can't handle this," she told him in all honesty.

He sighed roughly, smoothing back her hair. "I know. I sure as hell don't know what I'm going to do about it, either." He paused. "I don't know what's going on here. This isn't easy, Lissa. This business of wanting you—it's eating me up. I only meant to offer you and the baby some help."

"I've told you," she told him. "You're under no obligation."

He shook his head. "But it's not really that simple, is it?"

"What do you mean?"

"I mean, now that we have this other...problem to deal with. What are we going to do about it?"

"I don't know," she finally answered.

Dear Reader,

Happy New Year! And what a *fabulous* year it's going to be. First, due to *overwhelming* popular demand, we have another fun-filled lineup of *Man of the Month* books... starting with *Lyon's Cub* by Joan Hohl. In the future, look for *Man of the Month* stories by some of your favorite authors, including Diana Palmer, Ann Major, Annette Broadrick and Dixie Browning.

But Silhouette Desire is not only just *Man of the Month,* because each and every month we bring you six sensuous, scintillating, love stories by six terrific writers. In January, we have Jackie Merritt, Amanda Stevens (this is her long-awaited sequel to *Love is a Stranger* and it's called *Angels Don't Cry*), Kelly Jamison, Cathie Linz and Shawna Delacorte.

And in February we're presenting a special promotion just in time for Valentine's Day called *Mystery Mates.* Read and see how each Bachelorette opens the door to love and meets the Bachelor of her dreams. This promotion is so wonderful, we decided to give you six portraits of the heroes, so you can see each man up close and *very* personal.

Believe it or not, that's just what I have in store for you the first *two months* of 1993—there's so much more to come! So keep reading, enjoying and letting me know how you feel.

All the best,

Lucia Macro
Senior Editor

KELLY JAMISON

HEARTLESS

SILHOUETTE *Desire*®

Published by Silhouette Books New York

America's Publisher of Contemporary Romance

SILHOUETTE BOOKS
300 East 42nd St., New York, N.Y. 10017

HEARTLESS

ISBN: 0-373-05760-1

First Silhouette Books printing January 1993

Printed in the U.S.A.

Books by Kelly Jamison

Silhouette Desire

Echoes from the Heart #579
Hearts in Hiding #626
Heartless #760

KELLY JAMISON

grew up in a small town and often makes rural communities the settings for her books. She always knew that she wanted to be a writer. After her college graduation, she worked for a newspaper that was so tiny it didn't even have its own camera. Whenever a staff member needed to take a picture, he'd borrow a camera from the woman next door.

Kelly is a rabid chocoholic and pizza addict who also paints in watercolors and rides her bike. She has written as Kelly Adams.

One

___

Through the open door to the back storeroom, he could see her moving purposefully back and forth, loading a dolly with crates containing plastic milk cartons. Each time she passed by, the light caught the pure gold highlights in her long, blond hair. She looks like a golden butterfly, Joe Douglas thought. No wonder his brother had been so enamored of her. He continued to watch her, his distaste at the task that had brought him here evident on his face.

The other clerk, the one Joe had approached when he'd entered the store, said something to the woman. She frowned and glanced his way. Even from this distance he saw the deep blue of her eyes. Before he could catch himself, a momentary warmth enveloped him. But he forced himself to remember his brother, and the warmth passed.

Impatiently he looked at his watch, then at the paper bag he held in his hand. He had work to do, and he wanted to get this over with as soon as possible. It was an unpleasant chore, this meeting with Lissa Gray, and he wanted to get out of here and as far away from her as he could. A woman like Lissa Gray was a pretty flower with a deadly attraction, and he wanted nothing to do with her. If it weren't for Alex, he wouldn't even be here.

"I don't *know* who he is," Bonnie Ann said, casting a surreptitious glance at the man in jeans and workboots. "But if some tall, handsome sucker like that one came looking for me, I'd sure go see what he wanted. Maybe you won that Publishers Clearinghouse Sweepstakes."

"That's *not* Ed McMahon," Lissa said, pointing out the obvious. "And he doesn't look like he's at all happy about being here." She did a quick mental inventory of any bills that might have gone unpaid this month, but she thought she was caught up for once. Still, this guy looked like he wanted to shake *something* out of her, money or otherwise. From here, his eyes appeared almost black. Late-afternoon sun slanted through the glass door behind him, putting him in silhouette.

"Looks like the type who gets madder the longer he's kept waiting," Bonnie Ann suggested, her curly black hair bobbing around her face as she peered out for another assessment.

"Thank you very much for the encouragement," Lissa said dryly, wiping her hands on the green Duncans' Quik Shop jacket that all the clerks wore. "Here—see if you can get this milk out to the refrigerator without dumping it on the floor." She glanced at her watch. Almost six p.m., the end of her shift today.

Bonnie Ann gave an elaborate sigh at Lissa's assessment of her milk-delivering capabilities and pushed the dolly out the door. Lissa grinned, the smile fading as she turned and saw the stranger watching her. He looked vaguely familiar, but she couldn't quite place him.

"Yes, how may I help you?" she said as she stopped before him, again wiping her hands against her jacket. She had to look up to meet his eyes. Lissa was five feet eight, but this guy towered over her by another good half foot. This close she could see that his eyes were really a honeyed brown, slightly lighter than the hair that was just shaggy enough to give him a dangerously unsettling air. Dimly she realized he must be some kind of workman. His jeans, though clean, had obviously seen their share of time in the sun and dirt, as had his workboots. The black sweater looked newer—and expensive. It was the kind of upscale clothing she'd sold in her previous job at a menswear store.

"I'm Joe Douglas," he said tightly, his look taking her in and dismissing her at the same time.

It took a moment for the name to register, and then all the air seemed to rush out of her. "Joe Douglas," she repeated, recognition dawning. "You're... were... Alex's—"

"Brother," he finished for her, his dark eyebrows drawing together as the word dropped from his tongue like acid. The grooves on either side of his mouth deepened as he tightened his jaw.

No wonder he looked familiar. His hair was darker than Alex's had been, but he had the same eyes. She had only seen Joe once, just for a couple of minutes. She had gone into a restaurant with Alex and he had reluctantly introduced her to his older brother. *Alex.* Just thinking of him brought back the old anger.

"I'm sorry about Alex," Lissa said soberly, pulling together her composure. "I would have come to the funeral, but..."

"But your presence there would have violated even *your* principles," he finished again for her.

"Look," she said, flushing angrily. "I'm sorry about your brother. But if there's something you'd like to say, then say it. I've got better things to do than stand here and let you unload on me." She stared defiantly at him, finding an already bad day suddenly turning worse. She had spent enough sleepless nights blaming herself for getting involved with Alex Douglas without hearing it all over again from his brother. "How did you find me anyway?"

"The manager at your apartment back in Pittman told me you'd moved here to Petersburg." His tone was no warmer, but he had apparently reined his open hostility. "I found your address in the phone book and talked to your landlady. She said you were working here."

"All right. You've found me. Now what did you come for?" Lissa shot a glance at Bonnie Ann who had stopped stocking the dairy case to eavesdrop unabashedly.

He hadn't remembered how striking her blue eyes were, he thought, frowning. He had disliked Lissa Gray from the moment Alex had introduced her over a year ago, disliked her for levering herself between him and Alex, disliked her for causing Alex so much pain. She had disrupted Alex's life. But he found it wasn't so easy to maintain his carefully cultivated dislike when she was standing in front of him, her eyes wide and blazing, her waist tiny under a ridiculous green jacket that must be two sizes too big for her.

Remembering, he held up the paper bag. "I wanted to give you these." He pulled out a hardcover book of poetry and a framed photograph, shoving them toward Lissa.

She recognized the book as one she'd given Alex for his birthday. She turned over the photo and stared at it without comprehension. It was a picture of her standing by a car, looking serious, but it took her a moment to place the circumstances. She vaguely remembered Alex saying he needed to finish out a roll of film in his camera. Why wasn't she smiling? Had she and Alex fought that day? She really couldn't remember. Maybe time was a great healer, after all.

She had met Alex Douglas after she'd moved to Pittman, Missouri, to take a job managing a menswear store. He came into the store at Christmas to buy a tie, then came back the next day to ask her out. She dated him for five months before she found out two things almost simultaneously—she was pregnant and Alex was engaged to another woman at the same time he was seeing Lissa.

She had wondered afterward how long Alex had believed he could continue his deception. Perhaps he thought he would be through with Lissa before she found out. At any rate, she had gone to his house uninvited one afternoon, something she had never done before. She wouldn't have done it this time, but she had just returned from the doctor's office where she'd discovered she was indeed pregnant. She needed to talk to Alex right then.

She'd parked her car in the shade across the street and was about to get out when Alex's front door opened, and a leggy brunette came out, stopping to share a long kiss with Alex. When the woman came around to the driver's side of her car and reached for the door handle, the sun glinted off the engagement ring on her left hand. Lissa sat in the car for a long time after the brunette had left, and then she walked leadenly to Alex's door and confronted him.

He admitted it all too readily. Yes, he was engaged. He was sorry she'd found out. No, he'd just assumed he and Lissa would go on as they had before. After all, they'd never mentioned marriage.

Lissa did the only thing she felt she could; she broke off her relationship and resigned from her position at the store to move back to Petersburg, eighty miles away. She never told Alex about the pregnancy. Just before Suzanne was born seven months ago, Lissa read in the newspaper that Alex Douglas had been killed in a car accident. She still felt angry with Alex for deceiving her and angry with herself for being naive enough to be duped by a good-looking man.

And now Joe Douglas stood before her with the same eyes that had once enticed her into Alex's bed. Except that there was a smoldering anger in those eyes, anger directed at her. She supposed she knew what he must think about her relationship with his brother; certainly Alex would have bent the truth considerably to put himself in the best light. Alex was the kind of man who always attracted women. It was what she and Alex had fought about most—his shameless flirtations. But what Joe Douglas thought of her didn't matter.

And yet, when she looked into his honeyed eyes, it did matter, if only for an instant.

"Why did you bring me these?" she asked, not understanding what he was doing here.

He stared at her warily. "I was going through Alex's things, and I didn't want to take anything that was rightfully someone else's." He put the barest of inflections on *someone else's.*

She understood his carefully veiled insult immediately, and she felt color seeping into her face. Joe's disdain for her involvement with a man who belonged to someone else was like a slap.

Her fingers shaking, she turned the photograph over and slid the backing and picture from the frame. "Here," she said sharply, shoving the frame toward him. "I wouldn't want to keep anything that belongs to you."

"You don't have to—" he began, but she interrupted. "Take it!"

He felt a small measure of satisfaction at the stricken look on her face. She was angry, but she was also hurt, and he didn't regret his words.

Alex had once said that she was the kind of woman who could weave a spell around a man, and, even discounting Alex's propensity to embellish a woman's attractions, Joe realized that Alex hadn't been far off the mark. She was a beautiful, if deceptive, woman. Joe had made it plain from the moment he'd met Lissa over a year ago that he disapproved of the relationship. Alex had told him that Lissa was only interested in an affair of short duration. But by the time she dumped him, Alex was already so besotted with her that his fiancée realized there was someone else and broke off the engagement. From there Alex went downhill. His drinking increased, and the night his car ran off a curve, killing him, his blood alcohol level was well over the legal limit.

As far as Joe was concerned, his brother's tragedy was attributable to the woman in front of him, the woman who had wormed her way into his life and destroyed it.

Slowly he touched the frame, letting his fingers close over hers. He sensed her confusion as her fingers stiffened. He deliberately held her there, well aware of the unspoken challenge he was issuing. *Go ahead and try me, Lissa Gray. I'm not as easy as my brother.* The thought crossed his mind that it wouldn't be all that unpleasant to have her try her charms on him. He abruptly let her fingers go, and she pulled them away at once.

She was staring up at him, absently brushing her hand against her jacket. Guileless blue eyes studied him with more than a small amount of antagonism, making him wonder how unflattering her assessment of him was. He should leave right now, get out of the store and not look back. He'd done what he came to do, and if it included hurting Lissa Gray with his judgment, well, it was what she deserved. There was still the matter of the money his brother had owed her. Joe could drop a check in the mail, and then he would be done with Lissa Gray forever.

But something kept him rooted to the spot, intrigued with the seascape of her eyes as one emotion after another chased through them. He wondered what those blue eyes would look like when a man was making love to her. He figured she'd used her sexual charms to snag Alex, but it was still tempting to imagine her in his own bed, her slender body open to him.

Lissa recognized the frank interest on Joe's face, and it angered her even more. But before she could say anything, she became aware of Bonnie Ann hovering, clearing her throat and shifting her weight from one foot to the other. "Thank you for the book and picture," Lissa said with icy formality to Joe Douglas, dismissing him. He turned for the door, and Lissa breathed a sigh of relief to be rid of the man. "Well?" Lissa said to Bonnie Ann, her voice still sharp with annoyance reserved for Joe Douglas.

"The baby," Bonnie Ann prompted, rolling her eyes toward the counter. "You want to get her or should I?"

Lissa took one last look at Joe and disappeared behind the counter. Suzanne, in her infant carrier on the floor, grinned and flailed her chubby hands at the sight of her mother. The little girl's fretting immediately quieted. "Thought I'd left you here for Bonnie Ann, didn't you?" Lissa crooned to the baby, smiling back at her child's obvious pleasure. "Poor baby."

"Her Aunt Bonnie Ann spoils her enough," Bonnie Ann said over Lissa's shoulder, making faces at Suzanne while the baby babbled happily. "You go ahead and run along. Is Mrs. McGee watching Suzanne tonight while you're at class?"

Lissa nodded, picking up the carrier and diaper bag and backing toward the door. "See you later."

Lissa turned around to open the door and found herself about to plow into Joe's chest. Stopping short, she steeled herself for any other insult he might care to throw her way as a parting shot. At the same time she was vaguely aware of a breathlessness in her throat, a trip-hammer thudding of her heart that seemed out of all proportion to her juggling of the baby and diaper bag.

But he didn't say anything, just stared at her and the baby as though he was trying to put some puzzle pieces together. Lissa could see the question in his eyes, but she refused to answer it. Raising her chin a fraction of an inch, she pushed past him and shoved open the door with her hip.

She thought she heard him say something behind her, but she couldn't catch the words as she kept walking to her car.

Wait. It was the only thing he could think to say, and he didn't know what he would have said if she'd actually stopped. What would he do, interrogate her about her life, about why she'd given up a store manager's job to become a clerk, about her baby? That was what was bothering him, the baby. Frowning, he got into his pickup truck and stuck the key in the ignition. But he didn't start the engine. He was still sitting there five minutes later when Bonnie Ann glanced out the window.

Lissa couldn't seem to keep her mind focused on her errands, and she muttered under her breath as she started to push the cart into the grocery check-out lane, only to realize she'd neglected to pick up the very item she'd stopped for—orange juice. She could have gotten the juice at the store where she worked but this grocer carried larger quantity cartons, which was far more in line with Lissa's and the baby's demand for the stuff. The car died once on the way home, but providence was with her, and she got it moving again. Her budget didn't cover car repairs, either.

A half hour later Lissa pulled the car into the tiny, graveled parking area behind the apartment house and began unloading. May evenings in Missouri were lush with sound and scent, and Lissa paused a second to inhale the honeysuckle and appreciate the chorus of frogs.

"I'll carry the groceries and you get the cleaning," Lissa advised the baby, only to be rewarded with a drooling grin as Suzanne aimed a teething ring in the direction of her mouth. Lissa smiled and scooped up Suzanne, the bag of groceries and the wool coat that hopefully would get her through next winter, now that it was cleaned and repaired.

The house was a small brick two-storied building owned by Mrs. Polly McGee. When Lissa had inquired about renting one of the two upstairs apartments over a year ago, she had felt compelled to tell Mrs. McGee up front that she was pregnant. Mrs. McGee had taken Lissa's hand in hers, smiled and lowered the rent. The second apartment was badly in need of repairs and remained unoccupied, so Lissa had the upstairs entirely to herself. An iron balcony ran the length of the back, and Lissa loved to sit on it in the evenings with the baby. Mrs. McGee adored Suzanne and was only too happy to baby-sit for less than minimum wage when Lissa was at work or class. The arrangement was perfect, like having an on-premises grandmother.

Lissa had a place to stay, a baby-sitter and a part-time job that gave her the flexibility to work on her degree at the community college. There was just one bump in this road to paradise; most of the time Lissa didn't know if she was coming or going or running in place. At twenty-nine, she'd gladly shouldered the responsibilities of single motherhood. And no matter how tired she became or how many macaroni-and-cheese dinners she ate, she was damned if she was going to go to the Douglases for help. Alex may have been the baby's father, but to Alex that would have represented a liability. She was sure his family would feel the same way.

She was breathless by the time she'd negotiated the fifteen steps to the top floor. The stairwell was dark and slightly damp, but she knew it by heart and seldom bothered with the light. Which was why she shrieked when she rounded the corner of the banister and saw a shadowy figure.

Suzanne's eyes widened at her mother's outburst, and then she set up a steady wail.

Fear gave way to irritation as Lissa recognized Joe Douglas. "What are you doing here?" she demanded with no small amount of indignation, gently jiggling the baby until the child's cries quieted. She'd had enough of the man, and finding him on her doorstep was the last straw.

"I'm not exactly a bag of yesterday's garbage that someone left in front of your door," he said defensively.

Lissa merely raised her brows and turned away.

He'd remembered from long ago how elegant she was, but not this remote, inaccessible air she seemed to have acquired.

She put the baby carrier on the floor, then jammed her key in the lock and tried to ignore him, which was hard when he kept stepping into and out of the tiny pool of dwindling light from the window in the hall. Apparently he was as agitated as Lissa. Gritting her teeth, Lissa tried once again with the key and said, "Will you *please* stand still!"

"What for?" he asked suspiciously.

"Because I can't possibly open this door with you dancing in my light every two seconds."

He stood still then, looking abashed, then impatient, until Lissa nudged the door open with her hip and deposited her armload of groceries and cleaning on the kitchen table. Still holding Suzanne possessively in her arms, she turned on Joe.

"Now, what are you doing here?"

"Your friend—the clerk at the store?"

"Bonnie Ann," Lissa prompted him.

"Yeah, her. The one with the dark hair. Drinks coffee and talks nonstop. She came out and told me you'd left this on the counter." He held out Lissa's history book.

"What did she give it to you for?" Lissa asked, suspicious.

"How should I know?" His impatience was growing. He never should have come here. "Maybe she thought we were friends." At Lissa's raised eyebrow, he shrugged.

Lissa tightened her lips and tried not to look too hard at Joe Douglas, which was becoming increasingly difficult. She wondered briefly if he knew how attractive he was. He was handsomer than Alex, and Alex had fancied himself irresistible.

She took the book from him, careful this time to keep her fingers well away from his, and set it on the table. She stood waiting expectantly, and he could see her bracing herself for whatever he might say. He should just give her the money Alex owed her and get the hell out. He didn't understand what was making him prolong this, unless it was the way his blood heated whenever she lifted those shuttered blue eyes to his.

"You're in school?" he asked, nodding toward the book.

"At the community college."

After another brief silence, he said. "What are you studying?"

"Whatever it takes to get a teaching degree," she said dryly. "Which at the moment includes American history and English lit."

The conversation, though Lissa thought of it as a continuation of their confrontation, lagged again. She was still standing, arms folded, and she hadn't offered him a chair. "Thank you for the book," she said curtly. "And now you're probably anxious to be on your way."

But he didn't move, just stood in her kitchen and stared back at her, his hostility unmistakable. She wanted to turn her back on him, but Lissa found that she couldn't look away. The honeyed light in his eyes, full of his own irritation, was hypnotic. She mentally calculated what little Alex had said about his older brother and decided Joe must be about thirty-five. And far handsomer than Alex. He had a hard, virile quality in his face and body that must attract women like bees to honey.

Don't think about him like that, Lissa's inner voice warned. You're not falling under another Douglas's spell. Joe Douglas was no doubt as spoiled and unprincipled as his brother. He was standing here in her kitchen because he wanted something from her. But she wasn't cooperating— whatever it was he wanted, she was having none of it. Abruptly tearing her gaze away from Joe's face, Lissa focused on the baby, settling her into her high chair. Then she walked over to the counter to prepare dinner.

For a moment, Joe surveyed her in silence. She was obviously working hard to keep him at arm's length—no, make that the length of the proverbial ten-foot pole. She didn't want anything to do with him, and he didn't quite understand. He'd thought she'd be conciliatory at least. *He* was the wronged party here, the man whose brother's life fell apart because of Lissa Gray. But she wasn't making any apologies, and Joe could feel his temper rising.

Forcing himself to rein his anger, he sat down on a chair and watched her move quickly and efficiently at the counter. "What do you do, drag the baby with you to class and work?" he said sardonically.

"Mrs. McGee, my landlady, baby-sits for me," she said, and he wouldn't have guessed that his question perturbed her in the least, except for the sudden clenching of her hand on a cupboard door. "Does that meet with your approval?"

Without waiting for an answer, she stuck a can of soup under the can opener and then pulled a pan off the set of hooks over the sink.

He frowned and leaned forward, drawing his legs back until he could rest his forearms on his knees. He was finding it difficult to maintain his perspective around her. He'd brought his finely honed anger to vent on her, and he'd expected her to cave in under it and at least pretend to be remorseful. She was a beautiful woman with a baby, a job and a class schedule. And she apparently had a heart of stone.

He became aware of the overly rapid ticking of a clock somewhere in the small kitchen as he answered slowly and deliberately. "What you do with your baby is no concern of mine. I'm here to build the new bridge connecting Petersburg with the highway across the river. Since I was going to be in town anyway, I figured..." He shrugged, letting the sentence trail away.

"You figured you'd come look me up and let me know exactly how you rate me as a human being?" She hadn't turned around from her work at the stove, but he heard the bitter edge to her voice, like frost tipping the last grass of summer.

"Something like that," he allowed, intrigued by the set of her shoulders, the swift marshaling of her defenses. The lady could take care of herself—she might as well wear a neon sign declaring that fact. Her stance advertised it, as did the tone of her voice and the unflinching way she continued fixing soup. It was as if she was waiting for him to strike out at her verbally, and she was bracing herself. She turned around only when Suzanne began to whimper. Joe was struck by the suppressed emotion in her eyes. Go ahead and get it over with, they said. She was obviously expecting him to continue his verbal attack on her, and she was working hard to maintain her defiance.

"Look," she said, picking up the baby and jiggling her. "Don't you have a boss waiting to hear from you tonight?"

He shook his head. "No boss. I own the company. And I'm not leaving until we get some things settled."

Owns his own company, she thought. Well, that certainly explained the expensive sweater. And his attitude. He was obviously used to having things his way. He also seemed determined to push her until she lost her composure.

"As far as I'm concerned, there's nothing to settle," she snapped. "If you have some more insults you'd like to utter, maybe you could write them down instead. I'll read them later and save us both some time. And now, if you'll excuse me, I have a baby who needs changing."

Lissa refused to stand and argue with him. She couldn't very well physically throw him out of her apartment; the last thing she needed now was to tangle with him on his own terms. So, she simply picked up the baby and carried her to the bedroom off the kitchen.

A terrible thought struck her as she put the baby down on the bed and drew the diaper pail closer with her foot. What if his preconceived notions about her included the assumption that she was one of those women who was available to any man? What if he was here for a little tumble in the sack with his brother's ex-lover? Would a man who seemed to dislike her so much really be interested in getting her into bed?

She wasn't at all reassured when she heard his voice at the doorway. "Was money the reason you dumped Alex?" he demanded.

"What?" she said, turning in surprise at the question.

"Alex borrowed money from you," he said harshly. "I found the canceled checks in his records. Was that it? He wasn't a good enough meal ticket to satisfy you?" He glanced derisively around the small apartment. "If you went looking for greener pastures, you didn't do very well. You should have set your greedy little sights on me instead of Alex."

Lissa pulled up the baby's plastic pants over the clean diaper, trying to quell her temper before she answered him. When she did, her voice was cool and controlled, a far cry from the angry turmoil roiling inside her. "I don't go looking for *meal tickets,*" she said in a low, even voice. "And if I decided to do that, I certainly wouldn't set my sights or anything else on you."

"No?" he asked softly, remembering the look on her face when his fingers had held hers on the photo frame. "Maybe you ought to think again."

His eyes locked with hers, challenging her, and she stared back, so angry she could have hit him.

It was the smell of burning soup that finally broke through to her brain, and she quickly snatched up the baby and hurried to the kitchen, relieved to be out of his presence. She didn't care what Joe Douglas thought of her. He'd come here to heap his condemnation on her, and she could live with that. What she couldn't abide was any attempt on his part to touch her. She'd been weak where Joe's brother was concerned, and she knew deep inside that Joe could be an even more irresistible force than his brother if he set his mind on it.

She could feel his eyes on her when he followed her into the kitchen, and she deliberately kept her back to him as she tried to salvage the burning soup.

"What's the baby's name?" he asked abruptly, and she stiffened. It was what she'd feared since he'd shown up here, questions about the baby.

"Suzanne," she said, buttering the bread for a grilled cheese sandwich.

"How old is she?"

She hesitated, then said, "Seven months."

"She has your hair."

And her father's eyes, Lissa thought. The bread sizzled as she laid it in the hot skillet, and she felt the sound hissing through her veins as she turned around to face Joe. "She's well taken care of," she said defensively.

"On limited resources," he said dryly, his glance encompassing the tiny kitchen. "Is that why you use cloth diapers? Because you can't afford the disposable ones? Surely it's a lot more work."

It surprised her that he'd noticed, but then, she should have guessed that he was scrutinizing every aspect of her life and finding her lacking.

"It's extra work," she allowed, "but Mrs. McGee has a washer and dryer in the basement. I keep some disposables for the times we're away from the house." She fixed him with an arch stare. "Anything else you'd like to know? My income, health history, maybe my moral views?"

"I already know all about your morals," he said sharply, and Lissa felt herself paling. She'd invited that remark, but her own anger rose swiftly.

"I know what you think I am," she said with as much control as she could muster. "And frankly, I don't care. As far as I'm concerned, there's nothing more to be said between us. I want you to leave, and I don't ever want to see you again. Is that clear enough for you?"

"That's fine with me," he shot back. "Here's a little parting gift that ought to sweeten your mood." He pulled some dollar bills from his pocket and threw them on the table.

"What's that?" she demanded suspiciously.

"It's the money you gave Alex. A hundred dollars. Your due."

"I don't want your money," she said coldly. Alex had borrowed the money from her shortly before she found out about his fiancée. He'd needed it to make a car payment, he'd said.

She crossed to the table in two strides, snatched up the money and threw it against Joe's chest. Startled, he caught it and stared at her. Without another glance at him, she swiveled away.

Joe bit off a sharp retort. He had to admit that he'd postponed giving her the money just so he could come to her

apartment and see how she lived. Well, he'd seen it. It was
obvious she needed the money, but the woman was too defiant to take it. Damn her and her acid tongue. It irritated
him even more that in spite of his personal antagonism toward her, he still felt a definite sexual hunger every time he
looked at her. He was torn between conflicting emotions. He
wanted to shake her for her perversity and at the same time
he wanted to touch her with his mouth there at the pale hol-
low of her throat while he ran his hands through her incredible golden hair. He could feel his belly clenching just
thinking about how she'd feel and taste.

He suppressed a snarl as he thought of what Alex had
gotten him into now. He'd been furious with Alex when his
brother had casually asked him to straighten out his check-
book several months ago, even more furious when he'd
found the canceled check from Lissa. And now he was furious with himself for returning the money in such a stupid
way. He should have mailed it to her and avoided ever seeing her in person.

A knock on the door interrupted his self-recriminations.
"Hello, hello!" came a voice he recognized as Lissa's landlady.

"Come in, Mrs. McGee," Lissa called, briefly looking
into Joe's face as she moved past him to open the door. She
glanced at her watch and groaned. "Oh, heavens! I'm late!"

Mrs. McGee came inside in a swirl of lilac cologne, her
pink polyester slacks and print blouse encasing an ample
figure. She didn't seem at all surprised to see Joe, just took
the baby from Lissa and smiled at him. "Well, hello, Mr.
Douglas. I see you found Lissa."

"Yes, I did." *And I wish to hell I'd never set eyes on her
again.*

Lissa was running around the room, turning off the stove
and gathering up a notebook and some books. "I've got to
run!" she called to Mrs. McGee as she bolted for the door.

"There's some soup on the stove and a grilled cheese sandwich if you're hungry. I'm sorry it's all a little burned. Suzanne ate about two hours ago."

She was out the door the next instant, and Mrs. McGee was still smiling placidly at Joe. "Well, *that* sounds tasty, doesn't it?" she said, looking quite sincere.

Joe didn't answer. He nodded to her and took off after Lissa. He caught up to her at her car.

When she heard his footsteps on the gravel, she turned with a worried look. He'd skirted the question long enough. He finally asked what had weighed on his mind since he'd left the convenience store.

"Who's the baby's father?"

Two

Lissa sighed as she realized her English lit class had just been dismissed. She'd hardly heard a word of the lecture. Now she'd have to wade through *Lord Jim* with no guide to the symbolism but her own imagination, which had been working overtime since Monday night when she'd stood frozen as Joe Douglas asked her who Suzanne's father was.

He knew.

Of course he knew. He wasn't stupid. Given Suzanne's age, he had to know. And it didn't help that Lissa had stared at him without answering, then slammed the door of her car and taken off in a rain of gravel.

She'd expected him to call or show up last night, and she'd gone to the library after work to avoid him. When she picked up Suzanne at Mrs. McGee's, the older woman had told her that Joe *had* been around. No, he didn't say what he wanted.

And Lissa wasn't sure she wanted to know what he wanted. She didn't want any Douglases in her baby's life, and Joe had made it quite plain what he thought of her. She wished he would go back home and leave her and Suzanne in peace.

"Lissa, have you gone comatose on me?" an impatient voice demanded. "I've been talking to you for two minutes now, and all you've done is stare into space."

Lissa looked up to see Bonnie Ann standing over her desk, frowning. "Sorry," she said, closing her notebook and standing. "I've had something on my mind."

"It wouldn't be that long-legged dream in jeans, would it?" Bonnie Ann probed with a hopeful smile.

"He's more of a nightmare. And I don't have a single note to help me wade through *Lord Jim.*"

"No problem. I'll type up an extra copy of mine for you." She pirouetted and tossed her empty coffee cup into the trashcan.

That was one blessing about having a friend hooked on caffeine, Lissa thought as they walked down the hall. Bonnie Ann needed plenty of activity to burn up her energy, and she was always more than happy to provide extra notes or a tasty casserole or a wake-up call in the morning.

The lingering warmth of the spring evening enveloped them as they pushed open the heavy door, and Lissa stopped and closed her eyes, inhaling deeply. "I feel like walking home tonight," she said, her eyes still closed.

"What a coincidence," said a male voice. "So do I." Lissa's eyes flew open to see Joe standing at the bottom of the steps, his hands in the pockets of his black leather jacket.

Lissa stood speechless, attributing the sudden thudding of her heart to the shock of seeing him there. Bonnie Ann bounded down the steps with all the exuberance of a twenty-five-year-old after three cups of coffee. "Hey, this is great, isn't it, Lissa?'' she called back up the steps. "Really, great, right? Huh?"

Lissa slowly descended the steps, Joe's gaze never leaving her face. Tonight his eyes were the color of apple cider. "I think I'd better ride with you, Bonnie Ann," she said. "I should get home and start reading the assignment."

Bonnie Ann looked from one to the other, from Lissa's pensive face to Joe's solemn one. She shook her head. "Listen, I've got to stop at the store and get some cocoa. I'm making a cake for my neighbor's birthday. And if I hurry, I can get to the fabric store before it closes and get a zipper for that evening dress I'm making. And I've got to get the car washed and waxed on the way home, too. You'd better walk, Lissa. See you later!" She waved cheerily and set out at a jog for the parking lot, leaving Lissa to stare after her mournfully.

"Is she really going to do all that?" Joe said at last, and Lissa looked at him. One dark eyebrow was quirked in disbelief, the crook of his mouth suggesting the same bemusement.

"Oh, yes," Lissa assured him. "She's a regular Betty Crocker from Hell."

For the first time, Lissa saw the beginning of a smile on Joe's mouth, but he quickly stifled it. Still, it made her heart start that ridiculous jumping again, like a skittish colt on a spring romp. His mouth was gorgeous! Full and inviting and . . . as reckless as a moonlight walk in May.

Lissa fell into step beside him, grateful that she had at least stopped staring. But she was still uncomfortably aware of his warmth and slightly musky smell so close to her. His legs were long, and she had to walk quickly to keep up, until he apparently noticed her effort and slowed.

She stole a sideways glance at him and saw the creases around the corners of his eyes and the laugh lines at his mouth. Funny. He didn't seem like a man who laughed much. But then, he hadn't sought her out for humor. Quite the opposite.

They walked two blocks without speaking, and Lissa hugged her arms to herself, more in effort to ward off the questions she knew he'd ask than to keep herself warm.

"Hey," he said suddenly, stopping in his tracks. "Why didn't you say you're cold?"

"I'm not—" she began, but he cut her off.

"Lissa, you're cold," he announced in a voice that brooked no argument. He was shrugging off his jacket. "Here." He held it up to help her into it, and when she didn't move, he handed it to her. Slowly Lissa drew on the jacket, accepting its warmth and the lingering male scent.

He stopped in front of the local coffee shop and nodded his head toward the open door. "I don't know about you, but I could use something to drink."

Lissa felt as though she could use something stronger than coffee, but she walked ahead of him into the shop.

Joe's hand came to rest on her arm as he guided her to a booth, creating a ripple of pleasure that almost made her sigh out loud. She hadn't felt such a rush of heat since...

Since Alex Douglas had walked into her store and touched her arm just like this.

Abruptly Lissa pulled her arm from Joe's grasp, covering the action by opening her purse. She slid into the booth, and he sat opposite her, his eyes never leaving her face.

"I'll pay," he said sharply. "No need to check your finances." His hand reached out to halt her fumbling fingers but stopped short of touching her. Lissa looked up at him and froze. His face was filled with anger, his dark brows knitted together and lips tightened. His eyes were like the muddy waters of a rain-pelted river.

"It's only coffee," he said coolly. "You won't be indebted to me for a cup of coffee." There was a caustic edge in his voice, and Lissa saw that Joe understood that she didn't want to owe the Douglases anything. He understood, and he condemned her for it.

She finally tore her gaze from his and pretended to read the hand-lettered sign displayed over the counter, listing the daily specials. When the clerk smiled brightly and asked what they wanted, Joe ordered two cups of coffee. "Have you had dinner?" he asked Lissa suddenly.

She was surprised at the question, but she nodded. "I grabbed something at home before class."

"Well, I haven't," he said. He ordered a double hamburger and an order of fries, then glanced at Lissa. "Bring her a hamburger, too," he said.

The waitress was gone before Lissa could protest.

"I doubt if you had time for anything resembling a decent dinner," he said, anticipating her argument.

He was right, *something* had been a glass of milk. But she wasn't going to admit that. "I'm not hungry," she insisted. "And I should be going." She glanced at her watch, but she was too unfocused to register what time it was. Joe Douglas was adept at keeping her off balance, and it wasn't a sensation she enjoyed.

But before she could move, the waitress was back with a pot of coffee and a small pitcher of milk. Lissa wouldn't look at Joe. She could feel Joe's tension mounting, and she felt suddenly claustrophobic in the booth. She needed to get back out in the fresh air and clear her head. She could feel her blood pounding in her temples.

She looks tired, Joe thought. What with her schedule and finances, she probably didn't eat properly. He watched her sweep her hair back with one hand, and again he felt that gnawing hunger for her in the pit of his belly. He forced his mind back to the matter that had made him seek her out tonight. He wasn't sure how she'd take the news. He couldn't decide whether he should lead up to it or just tell her outright.

He pulled a piece of paper from his pocket and shoved it across the table at her. "I called a diaper service," he said, deciding on the direct route. "They'll deliver the first batch to your apartment in two days."

"What?" Incredulity, and then outrage swept across her face.

He went on as though she hadn't spoken. "They'll bring you a set number of clean diapers—I've got it written down here somewhere—and then come by to get the dirty ones. It's all on the paper here." He pushed it closer when she didn't touch it, but she just continued to stare at him incredulously.

"I don't want any diaper service," she said at last, and he heard the contempt in her voice. "And I can't very well afford one."

"I'm paying for this," he said. "It won't cost you anything."

"Are you sure it won't?" she goaded him. "Just what is it you want?"

It was a good question and one he wasn't prepared to answer. The more he looked at her the more he wanted to touch her. She was beautiful and he was more than a little attracted to her. She could go far to relieve the tedium he'd face with the long construction job ahead of him. But he sensed that as much as she needed help and money, she wouldn't accept it gladly from him. And that galled him. Furthermore, he still felt that she hadn't paid her due where his brother was concerned.

Further argument was impossible as the waitress brought their hamburgers. Joe smiled politely, glad for the interruption. Maybe Lissa would calm down by the time the woman left.

No such luck.

"You had no right to do this!" she whispered angrily as soon as the waitress ambled back to the counter. Her hands were clenched on the edge of the table.

"Right has nothing to do with it," he said calmly, taking a bite of his burger. "You need some help."

"Not from you I don't."

"You've made that abundantly clear," he said drily. "But it doesn't change your circumstances."

"I don't have any problems with the way I live," she said. "What bothers me is why you're doing this."

He shrugged. "Because of Alex. You meant something to him once. I figure he'd want me to do this at least. To make things a little easier for you."

"I don't need you making things easier," she snapped. "I don't need you doing anything for me."

He would have retorted, but the angry desperation in her eyes stopped him. She was afraid of him. He could see it there in her face, no matter how hard she tried to hide it from him. He wondered why she was so upset, but he decided to let things drop for the moment.

"Eat your dinner," he said, nodding toward her plate. "We can have a fight later in a more private place, if you want."

She stared at him a long moment, then slowly glanced around the room. Only two other tables were occupied, but both couples were staring at them curiously, their attention apparently attracted by the sound of the argument. Forcing her eyes back to the table, she picked up the hamburger and took a bite. She was too upset to eat, but she had to do something to occupy her hands.

She barely touched any of the burger, Joe noticed, but at least she wasn't spitting defiance at him while he ate. In fact, she was silent, her eyes fixed moodily on the table.

Lissa didn't trust herself to look at him. Her emotions were in enough turmoil as it was. As much as she hated what he represented—the Douglas male arrogance and its attendant callous indifference to her feelings—she couldn't help the small shiver of desire that stirred in her blood every time his eyes met hers. This would be so much easier if he wasn't so handsome, if his deep gravelly voice didn't make her wonder how he would talk to a woman in his bed. She'd been without a man since she'd first found out she was pregnant, and celibacy must have made her particularly vulnerable to good-looking men with cold hearts.

They kept a careful distance between them as they left the shop, and Lissa still didn't look at him. The night air was cool on her flushed skin, and slowly the pounding in her head eased.

As Joe and Lissa were approaching the alleyway to the house, they passed a heavily scented wisteria weighted with dew when Joe spoke. "The reason I'm trying to help you out a little is because I think Alex was in love with you," he said quietly, and Lissa was so stunned that she stopped short and turned to stare at him. He looked angry, as though what he'd just said was more than just a passing observation. He had apparently thought long and hard to reach that conclusion, and the knowledge had apparently only fueled the disparagement he felt for her.

Joe looked down at the troubled blue eyes that stared back at him. He had been at war with his emotions ever since he'd set eyes on this woman. One look at her, and desire blazed through him as swiftly as the blink of an eye; one fleeting memory of his brother, and his anger burned just as quickly. He wanted to hold her, he wanted to touch her and he wanted to put as much distance between them as he could. He wanted the impossible.

Lissa willed herself not to tremble as she watched the fire burn in his eyes. *He hated her.* She could feel it in the intensity of his gaze and the taut hostility of his stance. He'd jammed his hands into his jeans pockets, and she could sense that they were tightened into fists.

"Whatever your brother may have felt for me ended a long time ago," Lissa said sharply, her rising anger making her voice unsteady.

"Isn't that what you wanted to hear?" Joe demanded harshly. "Or didn't it matter if Alex loved you or not? My brother's dead, in no small part because of the havoc you wreaked in his life. And you don't give a damn," he finished coldly. He knew he had pushed her too far when he saw the quick movement of her arm. He made no move to stop her, and Lissa's palm cracked across his cheek.

"You self-righteous son-of-a-bitch," she said from between clenched teeth. She raised her arm to hit him again, and Joe saw the glistening tears in her eyes.

This time he caught her arm, strong fingers closing over her wrist. "I deserved the first one," he said quietly, suddenly aware of her harsh, angry breathing.

He shouldn't have touched her, he warned himself. He shouldn't have seen the tears in her eyes.

Unable to stop himself, he drew her nearer. When his other hand moved to the back of her waist, pulling her even closer, Lissa flinched as though he were about to hit her. She stood immobile and unyielding, her chin tilted up defiantly.

She could feel his fingertips pressing through the leather of his jacket and her blouse. The wisteria's perfume became more intense as her senses sharpened with his nearness. He held her only inches from his chest, and though his grip on her wrist was unrelenting, she didn't think she could move even if he released her.

His face lowered towards hers, and before Lissa's lids closed heavily, she saw the fire in the depths of his dark eyes. Whether it was passion or anger she didn't know.

His mouth pressed hard against hers at first, then almost immediately gentled, caressing and coaxing until her lips parted on a groan. She could taste the coffee on his tongue as it probed her mouth, teasing her lips and tongue. She ached inside with a sweetness that was like a bubble of nectar bursting. The honeyed liquid throbbed in her belly, then seeped into her veins and traveled to every corner of her body. She could have wept with the force of the spell it cast on her, and she shuddered as the heat and sweetness raced down her spine.

She was surprised to realize that he'd brought her right hand, the one she'd struck him with, to his chest and released it, and she had no desire to move it. Her left hand crept up to join it.

He was beguilingly virile and he was Alex's brother, a combination that terrified her, but she didn't want him to stop kissing her. Beneath her fingers, his heart beat forcefully, and she found her hand caressing a pattern over its rhythm, illicit images creeping into her mind of another rhythm, the rhythm of a man making love to a woman. She kissed him back without reserve, her own hunger surprising her.

She had to stop thinking of Joe Douglas in her bed, but as his mouth ravaged hers yet another time, she couldn't seem to think of anything else. She wanted the man, no matter what he thought of her or her motives.

Lissa was dazed when Joe raised his head and stared down at her. His eyes, lit only by the street light's glow, were shadowy and smoldering, like a pool of black water, endlessly deep and filled with danger.

"I'm not Alex," he said, his voice harsh in the still night air.

Lissa snapped out of her trance as his words sank home. It wasn't an apology. It was a challenge. *I'm not Alex. You won't find it so easy to catch me.*

She looked down the alley at the back steps leading to her apartment and drew herself together. Turning back to Joe, she slipped off his jacket and handed it to him. "Thank you for the hamburger," she said, controlling the shaking of her voice. "Good night." Desire and anger surging through her, she walked toward the steps.

He stood awkwardly on the sidewalk and watched her go, feeling frustrated. He didn't trust her, he didn't want to become involved with her, and yet he could barely keep his hands off her.

He looked over his shoulder when he heard the squeak of wheels on the concrete and saw Mrs. McGee pushing a stroller toward him. She stopped and peered at him a moment, then smiled and came closer. "Ah, Joe, lovely night for a visit, don't you think?"

"Nice to see you again, Mrs. McGee," he said politely, unable to focus his attention on the older woman. He couldn't keep himself from glancing again at Lissa's retreating back.

Mrs. McGee followed his gaze. "Joe," she said suddenly. "Why don't you help me get the baby and this stroller upstairs." She smiled broadly. "I've been shopping," she confided, nodding brightly toward the thick bag in the large pocket at the back of the stroller. "Lissa!" she called, waving.

Lissa turned and hesitated before walking back toward Mrs. McGee. Resolutely, she avoided looking at Joe. "Did you and Suzie have a good walk?" she asked, trying to smile, but hearing the strain in her own voice, nevertheless.

"A dandy walk," Mrs. McGee confirmed, picking up the baby, who was kicking and smiling and holding her arms out for her mother. "I stopped at the drugstore and found some real treasures on the half-price shelf." Mrs. McGee winked at Joe as she pulled her bag of treasures from the stroller.

"Now, Joe, you know how to fold one of these things, don't you?"

Lissa allowed herself one look at Joe and saw that he was watching her. She didn't want him in her apartment again, but she could see from the set of his jaw that if she objected, it would only make him more determined. Her resistance to him seemed to irritate him more than anything else did. She tightened her mouth, but she kept silent.

"I see you've had experience with these contraptions before," Mrs. McGee said approvingly as Joe quickly folded the stroller and picked it up.

"It's been a while," he admitted, and Lissa could feel him still watching her as she started for the back steps. "I have a ten-year-old son," he added.

Lissa heard him, but she kept walking stiffly, jiggling the baby, who was babbling over her shoulder at Mrs. McGee. He had a son, she repeated in her head. Did he have a wife, too?

"I've been divorced for a long time," he said to Mrs. McGee, but Lissa knew the explanation was for her benefit. "Jay lives with my mother when I'm on a job, but . . . I have him with me when we can both work it out. His mother rarely has him over for a weekend let alone any substantial period of time."

Mrs. McGee clucked sympathetically.

Lissa turned on the light in the stairwell in deference to Mrs. McGee's weaker eyesight and went up ahead of them, hearing Mrs. McGee murmuring excitedly to Joe about the wonderful things she'd purchased. She could still feel Joe's eyes on her.

But Lissa wouldn't look at him until they were inside her apartment and the baby was comfortably ensconced in her infant seat on the kitchen table. What she saw troubled her. Joe's eyes were still sad and lonely. Perhaps it was from talking about his son; certainly it wasn't because of what he'd told her, that he wasn't Alex. Those words had come from anger, and it wasn't anger she saw now.

Seemingly oblivious to the tension between Joe and Lissa, Mrs. McGee eagerly emptied her bag onto the kitchen table near the baby and sat down. The bag had held five alarm clocks, and Mrs. McGee's eyes positively glowed.

"They were all half price!" she enthused, clasping her hands together. "And look, there's hardly anything wrong with any of them. This one's missing a hand, and this one has a broken leg." She was picking up each clock lovingly, as though each were a pet bird. "I'll have them back on their feet in no time at all!"

"Do you fix clocks?" Joe asked curiously as he pulled out the chair opposite hers. The mention of clocks reminded him of the low but frenetic ticking he heard again in Lissa's kitchen, but he still couldn't locate it.

"Oh, yes," she said reverentially. "It's been my hobby for a long time." She looked at Joe hopefully. "Do you have one that isn't working?"

Ignoring the sharp look Lissa gave him from her position at the counter, Joe shrugged. "Well, my watch has been running a little slow."

Lissa cleared her throat, and when Joe looked at her, she was giving him one of those you-don't-know-what-you're-doing looks that he got from his son, Jay, when he was naive enough to suggest that the boy might be tired and ready to go to bed. Joe had no idea what Lissa's look meant.

Mrs. McGee seemed to be in seventh heaven as she pocketed Joe's watch and assured him she'd have it fixed in no time.

"I used to sit on the front porch and work on clocks," she said, sighing. "But since the roof fell in and I had to tear the porch down, I work inside. I miss those summer evenings out there."

"It wouldn't take much to build a new one," he said.

Mrs. McGee shook her head. "Can't afford one," she said with a simple shrug. "Oh, I could afford the lumber, but not the labor. And my clock-fixing skills don't extend to carpentry."

Joe nodded slowly, his eyes drifting to Lissa. Lissa didn't know what was going through his mind, but she could read some intent on his face and it made her uncomfortable.

"Well, I certainly had a good time," Mrs. McGee said in satisfaction, carefully repacking her clocks. "Yes, indeed, a good time." She smiled at Joe, then bent down to stroke the baby's head. "Bye-bye, little one."

Suzanne grinned and kicked and reached out to Mrs. McGee. Lissa unstrapped her from her seat and picked her up, turning her so she could see her friend's departure. "Wave bye-bye," Lissa prompted, smiling as Suzanne took one hand from her mouth and obediently flopped it up and down. "Boo!" Suzanne cried in excitement.

"Boo to you, too," Mrs. McGee called fondly as she left.

"So tell me," Joe said after the door closed. "Will I ever see my watch again?"

She could still feel the demanding touch of his mouth on hers when he'd kissed her outside, and the memory of that haunted her. She was uncomfortable with the knowledge that he affected her that much, and she was wary of what else he might do—or ask.

"Oh, you'll get your watch back," Lissa assured him over her shoulder. "But I guarantee it will never run quite the same again." She turned around and pointed to a novelty clock on the back wall, nearly obscured by a hanging ivy plant. The clock was fashioned in the form of a cat. The eyes moved back and forth rapidly in tandem with the swinging tail. "That was one of Mrs. McGee's finds," Lissa said. "She 'fixed' it for me first. Notice anything odd about it?"

Joe studied the clock. "It runs a little fast, doesn't it?"

"It gains four hours each and every day," Lissa confirmed. "One of these days the eyes and tail are going to break the sound barrier."

Joe groaned.

Suzanne, entranced with the cat clock, stretched out from her mother's arms, fretting and on the verge of tears. Joe took her, while Lissa reached into the cupboard and brought out a teething biscuit to distract her. She held it in front of Suzanne and watched her eyes widen in anticipation before she curled her fingers around it.

When Lissa turned around, Joe was right behind her, and she drew up short. The warm male smell of his jacket came back to her in a rush, and she stared up into those enticing eyes. "You're avoiding me," he said. "We need to talk."

"There's nothing to discuss," she said quickly. "Please. Just leave. Leave us alone." She was pleading, asking him not to say what she knew was in his eyes.

He shook his head. "I can't leave you alone. I wish I could." He sounded resigned and infinitely weary. He released Lissa's wrist and handed over the baby who was murmuring softly. "I'm going now. But I'll be back. Make a list of anything you need for yourself or the baby and I'll take care of it for you."

Lissa's heart was pounding in her chest as he went to the door.

"Why?" she demanded when his hand was on the knob. "Why can't you just leave us alone?"

He turned and studied her in silence a moment, his eyes clouded with some emotion she couldn't read.

"Because you have my brother's baby."

His eyes held hers a second longer, and then he was gone. Lissa leaned back against the counter, oblivious to her daughter's chubby hand flopping in the air as she waved bye-bye.

Three

In Lissa's dream, a clock was striking in steady, ear-splitting thuds. It was trying to tell her something—in clock language, she supposed in that curious logic that rules dreams—and the message was urgent. It was something about Joe and Alex, but she couldn't quite decipher the meaning. A deep sense of sadness settled on her as she woke up. It was as though she was yearning for something, but she didn't know what it was.

Her head was filled with regret and aching slightly. The rhythmic thuds continued beyond her dream, and she pinpointed them in the vicinity of the house's front door. They sounded suspiciously like hammering.

Lissa sat up in bed and threw a peach-colored cotton robe over her short nightgown. Neither robe nor gown came below her knees, and she reached down, fumbling for the slipons she'd dropped beside the bed. More or less awake, she ran a hand through her hair and checked on Suzanne. The baby was still sleeping, her tiny mouth open and slack, her lashes dark and heavy against the silky cheek. Lissa felt a rush of love at the sight of her daughter, followed by an overwhelming sense of maternal protection.

Tiptoeing from the bay window in the cramped alcove that served as the nursery, Lissa tied her robe as she descended the back stairs. Delicately picking her way over loose gravel and grass badly in need of mowing, she peered around the corner of the house. She froze in her tracks when she saw Joe. No man had the right to look that good at this hour of the morning.

His jeans fit like a second skin, and as he knelt beside the foundation, his thigh muscles corded thickly beneath the fabric. His equally muscular back moved tightly against a red T-shirt. Dark brown hair curled at his neck, the rest falling in untamed waves.

Lissa's maturity and omnipresent unflappability had fallen somewhere around her ankles. She knew she was indulging in adolescent ogling, but she couldn't seem to stop. Her robe tie loosened as she took a deep breath to slow her pulse, and she held the robe shut with one hand.

Joe reached for a nail and glanced over his shoulder, stilling when he saw Lissa. For an instant, his eyes darkened like metal exposed to flame. She took a step backward, unnerved, coming to a stop as he stood.

"What are you doing?" she demanded when he continued to stare at her.

"Building a porch," he said grimly, gesturing with the hammer in his hand.

Lissa frowned. "Mrs. McGee can't afford a porch," she said.

"We've worked out an arrangement," Joe countered mildly.

"What sort of arrangement?"

Joe raised his brows. "I don't have to explain my book-keeping to anyone," he informed her.

"Just what are you getting in return for this porch?" Lissa pressed, sweeping her hand toward the pile of lumber on the ground and then clutching at her robe when it fell open.

Joe's mouth tightened, and it was a moment before he spoke. "I haven't gotten a spare key to your apartment, if that's what you're thinking," he said dryly.

"No?" Lissa said in growing agitation. The man was trying to insinuate his way into her life by using Mrs. McGee, and she resented it like hell. "Maybe if you build an attached garage, you can get the key."

"If I wanted the key," he said with cool assurance, "I wouldn't have to go to that much trouble."

Lissa sucked in her breath. "Your opinion of yourself is highly overrated," she snapped. "You need a dose of reality."

"Really?" He moved a step closer to her, and Lissa stifled her first urge to retreat. The day was sunny and warm, but his eyes were all shadows, as full of foreboding as an encroaching storm. "I think you're the one who has a problem with reality."

She would have turned and left then, but his hand snaked out and caught her arm, his fingers warm and firm on her bare skin below the sleeve of the robe.

"I've yet to hear you admit that my brother fathered your baby." The words, cool and clipped, made her flinch as though he'd sworn at her.

"You seem to have reached your own conclusions," she said, standing stiffly under his hand, her flesh burning where his fingers touched. "I can't imagine that you'd take my word anyway." She hated feeling such vulnerability when he was near her, hated knowing that her heart was hammering in her throat because the man was so damn good-looking that he could have had a hormone named after him. Her reaction was straight out of one of the fairy tales her grandmother used to read to her: the wicked princess who was cursed by a witch to find her worst enemy irresistibly attractive. Only Lissa couldn't think of herself as a princess, wicked or otherwise, and even a witch wouldn't have wished Joe Douglas on her.

"You're the one I want to hear say it," he told her, his eyes never leaving her face.

Lissa took a deep breath, refusing to look away from him. Trying for nonchalance, she shrugged. "All right. Your brother was Suzanne's father. Does that make you happy?"

Slowly he shook his head. "No, it doesn't make me happy. Why didn't you come to me? Or did you have another sugar daddy waiting in the wings?" The pressure on her arm had become softer, more seductive, and she had to quell the rising heat of her pulse, even as she fought to contain her anger. With deliberate disdain, she pried his fingers loose and jerked her arm away.

"It's obvious there's no sugar daddy here. And anyway, I wouldn't come to you for anything," she said with all the coldness she could muster.

"Careful, sweetheart," he warned her with a mocking smile. "You might have to eat those words someday. You're not in the ideal circumstances to raise a child, you know."

Lissa could feel the blood draining from her face. "What are you saying?" she asked hoarsely.

"Only that I have certain claims on Suzanne, and if I were you, I wouldn't push me too far. I have blood ties to her, and I definitely want a say in how she's raised. And if you try to stop me, I'll use every means at my disposal." He pinned her with a gaze as sharp as crystal. "You can't offer her nearly as much in the material sense as I can, and any court could see that."

Lissa quelled the shudder that had started down her spine. "Are you saying you'd try to take my baby away from me?"

"I think we understand each other," he said quietly, and she was tempted to hit him again. He was everything she detested, arrogant, underhanded and domineering.

"Then you're the one with no principles," she said in a low, even tone that belied her fury. Without another word, she spun away from him. She slowed her pace and composed her face only when Mrs. McGee poked her head out the front door.

"Lissa!" she called cheerfully. "Come down for dinner tonight. I've promised Joe that I'll fix a big meal, and you know how you love my fried chicken."

"I—I wish I could," Lissa stammered, trying to think of any reason why she couldn't. "But I have to work today, and I have a lot of studying to do tonight."

"Well, you just bring your books right along with you then," Mrs. McGee insisted. "That way you won't have to cook when you get off work."

Taking Lissa's silence for consent, Mrs. McGee nodded in satisfaction and closed the door.

Lissa could feel Joe's eyes on her, and she slowly turned around. She could almost hear him wondering how far to push her. Gradually she realized her hand had fallen from her robe, which now dangled open, exposing the thin cotton gown underneath. With the light behind her, she might as well have been wearing nothing. She saw Joe's gaze drifting down from her face. He lingered at the swell of her breasts before lowering to the bare expanse of leg showing where the robe ended. Her fingers felt suddenly stiff.

"I don't want to fight you, Lissa," he said, a new, gentler tone in his voice.

"You seem to be doing a good job, nevertheless," she said.

"I do what I have to do." He'd spoken the words quietly. But despite his tone, Lissa heard his determination, and she found herself wondering what weapons Joe Douglas would use. Probably the law. Probably bullying. But the weapon she dreaded the most was Joe himself.

She turned away, not wanting to look into his dark eyes any longer.

Lissa stepped gingerly onto the new flooring of the partially completed porch. She'd picked up Suzanne at Mrs. McGee's when she got off work. Now here they were at six-thirty on the dot, dressed and ready for dinner.

She took a deep breath, but nearly turned back when she reached Mrs. McGee's front door. She'd changed her clothes three times before she ventured out of her apartment, and now she was sure she should have made a fourth change. The white cotton skirt with its pattern of tiny pink flowers was too dressy. She should have worn jeans, just to show Joe that she didn't care how she looked for him. And she shouldn't have unbuttoned the top button of the short-sleeved pink blouse, even though it was more comfortable that way. She was also still wearing the mascara and blush she'd applied before work. She shifted the diaper bag in her hand and was about to leave when the door opened.

"So there you are," Mrs. McGee said cheerfully. The smell of fried chicken wafted through the open door, and Suzanne kicked and reached for Mrs. McGee. "Hello, sweetheart," Mrs. McGee cooed as she took the baby. "Come in now and see the lovely little bib I got for you."

"You shouldn't have," Lissa said, smiling at the older woman's obvious love for the baby, but Mrs. McGee pooh-poohed her mild protest with a wave of her hand.

Lissa followed her inside, stopping hesitantly at the kitchen doorway. Joe had been sitting at the cloth-covered round table, but now he stood. Lissa could feel his eyes on her as she set the diaper bag in the corner.

Lissa had seen less handsome men doing TV ads for men's cologne. Joe more than did justice to the khaki slacks and the lightweight blue sweater, both items no doubt costing more than she made in a week at Duncans'. Lissa found herself both wanting to stare at him in unabashed admiration and feeling disgust at her own weakness.

"Sit down, sit down!" Mrs. McGee ordered. Bouncing the baby on one hip, she checked the chicken, then pointed to the table. "Lissa, just look at the lovely flowers Joe brought. For heaven's sakes, I didn't get treated this well by Mr. McGee himself, God rest his soul."

A mason jar filled with daisies sat on the table, and Lissa's glance caught Joe's when she looked at the flowers. "They're beautiful," she said, looking away from him.

"Now," Mrs. McGee said, "You and Joe can work on this." She pointed to the hand-crank ice-cream maker on the floor. "Take it outside. I've got the rock salt there. When it's ready, we'll stick it in the freezer until it's time for dessert."

Lissa stared at her a moment, but Joe was already hefting the machine and heading for the front door. "Go on, shoo!" Mrs. McGee said. "I've got to finish this chicken."

Obediently, Lissa followed Joe. He didn't look at her when the door closed behind her, just picked up the bag of rock salt from next to the house and began pouring it into the machine.

Lissa looked around, then settled herself on the wooden platform that was apparently the floor of the porch-to-be. The sun was a flaming red ball sinking behind the trees, and in the distance she could hear a fledgling chorus of frogs. Mrs. McGee hadn't made ice cream in a long time, and Lissa knew she normally reserved the practice for visits from grandchildren. She thought it peculiar that Joe rated this kind of treatment. But then, he was building her a new porch.

Joe stopped working a moment to look over at her. Lissa tensed, half expecting him to renew his verbal attack on her.

"My dad loved ice cream," he said simply, turning back to the machine on the ground in front of him. "He took us out every Sunday for an ice cream cone." He smiled slightly, and Lissa uncurled her arms from around her knees. His voice sounded sad instead of angry, but she was afraid to ask him about his father.

"Mine took me out for milkshakes," she volunteered, watching him turn the crank. The machine slipped and Lissa stood. "Here, let me help." She knelt beside him and held the device steady while he turned. Her face was close to his, but she stalwartly kept her eyes down on his hands, strong hands with large knuckles. "Every Saturday night we'd leave the house right after dinner."

"A family tradition," he suggested.

"Oh, it was a tradition all right," she said thickly, looking down again. "Dad was a great believer in tradition." Lissa frowned and concentrated on holding the ice-cream maker steady. She hadn't meant to say so much. She hadn't talked about her parents to anyone in years.

Joe stopped cranking, and Lissa raised her head again, finding herself staring into hazy eyes. "What happened to your father?" he asked. "You sound very sad when you talk about him."

Something compelling in Joe's face made her answer him. "Part of the tradition was that on the way home from the ice-cream shop, we'd stop off at the tavern." She gave an eloquent shrug that belied years of pain. "We'd stay until the place closed. When I was five, my father died of a heart attack brought on by years of alcohol abuse."

"Surely your mother wouldn't let you spend night after night at a tavern," he said, frowning. "Besides, weren't you too young to be allowed in a tavern?"

"My mother had her own interests," Lissa said. "As far as the tavern owners were concerned, their livelihood depended on people like my mother to drop in regularly. So, I was part of the package."

"She didn't care?" He sounded incredulous.

"Ours was not a family straight out of a Norman Rockwell painting," she said dryly.

"But surely she cared about you," he insisted. He surprised himself with his need to know more about this woman. Despite everything—his brother, the baby—he was beginning to feel more than a passing interest in her.

"Look, this will only bore you," she said restlessly.

"Go on," he said. He'd begun turning the crank again, but his eyes were fixed firmly on her face. She'd seen his eyes turn judgmental and accusatory over the past couple of days, but now they were boring into her with an intensity that nearly made her tremble. She couldn't tell what he was thinking, but she felt she had to tell him the rest of the story. She didn't understand her sudden need to unburden herself on a man who disliked her so violently, but once she'd began the story, she couldn't seem to stop herself from continuing.

Lissa looked down at her hands again, realizing as she did how tense her body was. "Mom had to work because—well, Dad's life insurance coverage was far from adequate," she finished wryly. "Women generally didn't get good jobs in those days, and Mom didn't have a lot of schooling. So she worked long hours, and she was bone-tired when she got home." Her gaze shifted to his hands—large, beautiful hands accustomed to work. Her own hand, slim and pale, lay close to his, so close that she could have touched his hard fingers if she wanted. Lissa wrenched her thoughts back to her childhood.

Joe waited for what she was going to say, realizing that it was difficult for her. She had such troubled blue eyes, as though she was watching something painful unfold.

"She must not have had much time to spend with you," he prompted when she fell silent.

"No. She didn't." Lissa shrugged. "She sent me to live with my grandmother. I saw Mom for one hour every Sunday evening when she dropped by."

"One hour?" Joe asked incredulously.

"She was . . . living with someone," Lissa explained quietly. "He wasn't willing to marry her, but my mother needed him. My grandmother didn't approve, so she limited my mother's visits."

"That's criminal!" Joe said in disbelief.

"No," Lissa said, her eyes finding his and holding them. "As you so succinctly put it this morning, people do what they have to do." She stood up and carefully brushed off her skirt. "My grandmother would have done anything to protect me, and I can understand that. I'd do the same for Suzanne." She held his gaze, letting him read the resolve in her eyes, and then she gave a brief, bitter smile. "I'll go tell Mrs. McGee that you have the ice cream under control."

Joe stared after her in grudging admiration, the ice cream the last thing on his mind. He understood that Lissa was meeting his challenge. If he tried to take away her child, she'd do whatever she had to do to stop him. He understood all right, but if it came down to that, he was sure he'd win in the end.

Lissa was carrying a bowl of peas to the table when Joe came in with the ice cream. "Mission accomplished," he said cheerfully, his eyes lingering just a bit longer than necessary on Lissa.

"Lissa, will you help Joe get the ice cream into this bowl?" Mrs. McGee said as she bustled to the table with a plate of fried chicken. "I think we're almost ready to eat."

Lissa put the bowl on the counter, watching as Joe lifted out the ice cream paddles and rinsed them in the sink. "Here we go," he said, putting the machine on the counter and tilting it. Lissa began scraping out the chocolate ice cream with a large spoon, trying not to look at Joe. He upended the canister as she got at the last dabs of ice cream clinging to the sides, and his knuckles brushed her hand. Lissa stiffened and quickly finished her task. But after righting the canister, Joe reached out a long finger to wipe a drop of melted ice cream from her arm.

Lissa shivered slightly from the contact and drew her arm away. "Don't," she said in a low voice so Mrs. McGee wouldn't hear.

"Don't what?" he countered with raised brows. A moment of silence passed between them, the tension so taut that Lissa could feel it grating her nerve endings raw.

Over the pounding of her heart, she heard Mrs. McGee set Suzanne in the high chair and then enter the storage room off the kitchen.

Joe began rinsing the canister. "Your protests are a little hypocritical, don't you think?" he said sarcastically. "I can see what's written all over your face. And I feel the same thing. I'm not exactly happy about it, either, but it seems to be the one area where we're compatible. Maybe we should make the most of it."

Anger and resentment and outrage welled up inside her, and only Mrs. McGee's return kept her from giving vent to her feelings. Joe was like Alex, cocky and self-assured. A tiny voice inside her head mocked her with the knowledge that he was right, that his touch did incite a riot of pleasure within her. But she wasn't going to give in to it. Never again was she going to let herself be seduced into that trap: loving a handsome, lying man.

Lissa turned away from him and blindly put the bowl in the freezer. Mrs. McGee, fussing over the baby, apparently took no notice of Lissa's agitation. By the time they sat down to dinner, Lissa sitting across from Joe, Lissa's heartbeat was nearly back to normal.

Mrs. McGee plied them with a surfeit of food—green beans, coleslaw, spiced peaches, homemade biscuits and strawberry jam, and the fried chicken was indeed a culinary masterpiece. Lissa had little appetite and only picked at her food, but she saw that Joe was eating with relish.

After cooing over Suzanne and helping Lissa feed her some cereal, Mrs. McGee abruptly steered the conversation to Joe as they started on the ice cream.

"Joe," she said, poking her spoon in his direction. "How come a good-looking man like you's divorced?"

Lissa blanched and kept her eyes on her bowl.

"I know I'm too direct and not so polite," Mrs. McGee said, "but I'm getting old. I don't have the patience to wait to find out what it is I want to know."

"My wife and I had . . . some fundamental differences," Joe said carefully, his face a study in control. "She didn't want to work on our problems."

"That's too bad," Mrs. McGee clucked sympathetically. "It's so hard on the little ones when there's a divorce. You said you have a son?"

Joe nodded. "Jay. He's a great kid. Somehow he's survived what happened between his mother and me."

"Ah, kids," Mrs. McGee said. "They weather it all somehow, don't they? I had three sisters myself. Let me tell you, we were holy terrors. Always into everything. Do you have sisters, Joe?"

"No, ma'am. I . . . had a brother, Alex. He was killed in a car accident."

Lissa's throat was closing, and she swallowed hard. She stole a quick glance at Joe and saw his jaw tighten.

Mrs. McGee was apparently oblivious to the sudden tension at the table, because she said, "It's so sad to lose someone that way. Did he leave a wife and children?"

Joe was silent a moment before he said, "No, he was engaged to be married before the accident, but his fiancée broke it off. Alex was...drinking heavily before the accident. His death was the result of things gone wrong."

In the silence that followed, Lissa slowly raised her eyes and found Joe staring at her, his mouth compressed, his eyes brooding. In a way, he was right. Things *had* gone wrong, terribly wrong. But if she told Joe the rest of the truth, that she had known nothing of Alex's fiancée, she had no hope that he would believe her. This was his brother, and there were blood ties between them. Her word was a whisper in the wind next to Alex's, even in death.

"So sad," Mrs. McGee was murmuring. "So sad."

"Let's not talk about losses," Joe said, turning to Mrs. McGee. "I bet you have grandchildren, don't you?"

"Oh my, yes!" Mrs. McGee exclaimed, and she was off and running on that cherished topic.

Lissa slipped from her chair and quietly began clearing the plates and loading the dishwasher. Engrossed in family stories, Mrs. McGee hadn't noticed Lissa's lack of appetite. But when she looked back at the table, one person was watching—Joe, his eyes as implacable as when he'd talked about his brother. Lissa met his steel gaze and looked away.

Mrs. McGee was lamenting the departure of two of her grandchildren. "And then Everett was transferred out of state," she said. "So my daughter and grandsons had to move with him." She sighed. "I still have three granddaughters here, but darn that Everett! On top of that, he was planning on fixing up the apartment next to Lissa's before the move came up. So now I'm minus two grandchildren and I've still got an apartment unfit to rent.''

"The apartment's empty?'' Joe asked, a note of interest in his voice.

"The shower doesn't work, the tile needs replacing, the stove doesn't work, two windows are cracked and the toilet runs all the time.'' She sighed. "It's in worse shape than Mr. McGee was in before he died, God rest his soul.''

"I was looking for an apartment,'' Joe said slowly. "I haven't been able to find a motel around here that has rooms with kitchenettes and that rents by the month.''

"But this place—'' Mrs. McGee gestured toward the ceiling helplessly ''—it's not fit to live in.''

Lissa looked from one to the other apprehensively. Joe was talking about moving in right next to her. She'd see him every day, hear him in the apartment, see him constantly in the stairwell. She'd step onto the balcony, and he'd be there. She shook her head and opened her mouth, but no one was paying any attention to her.

"I think I could fix it up,'' Joe was saying. "I'll take a look at it later on.''

"Oh, that would be wonderful!'' Mrs. McGee enthused. "You could live in it rent-free in exchange for the repairs.''

Suzanne whimpered and then began crying in earnest, dropping her bottle onto the floor. Lissa was walking toward her when Joe stood and picked up the baby. "I can take her,'' Lissa said, but already Suzanne was quieting.

Joe wiped the tears from her cheeks with his thumb, his hand looking incredibly large next to the baby's face. Suzanne leaned her head back to inspect him, then apparently decided he passed muster as she rested her head against his shoulder, clutched his shirt in one tiny fist and poked her thumb into her mouth.

"It's her bedtime,'' Lissa said. "She and I are going to have to say our good-nights.''

A contented Suzanne grinned at her mother around her thumb.

"Thanks, Mrs. McGee, for the wonderful dinner," Lissa said as she picked up the diaper bag. Hesitantly, she reached for the baby.

"I'll carry her," Joe volunteered. "Thanks for having me to dinner, Mrs. McGee. I'll come by to look over your apartment first thing in the morning."

"Joe!" Mrs. McGee called as he started for the door. "Wait, I fixed your watch."

She pulled the watch from her pocket and handed it to Joe with all the pride of a master craftsman. Joe looked at the watch and gave a weak smile. "Thanks, Mrs. McGee. I sure appreciate this."

Lissa fell into step behind him as they left by the side door. They walked around the outside of the house in silence, Lissa lifting her face to the cool breeze blowing from the west and trying not to stare at Joe's broad back. He looked so strong and rugged carrying her daughter that he nearly took her breath away. His dark hair rippled in the breeze, and his broad back muscles tightened under the sweater. Suzanne, traitorous female that she was, cooed at him as she bounced along in his arms.

Joe was surefooted in the dark stairwell, finding his way easily. Lissa trailed behind, her fingers gliding over the cool wood of the banister and her eyes still fixed on Joe's back. Rising from the depths of the past came a dim memory: Alex walking ahead of her in the dark, his back rigid. They were coming back to Lissa's apartment from a late dinner one night. She was asking him why they'd left the restaurant so quickly, before she'd quite finished her coffee, and Alex had resented the question. At first he'd told her he'd grown restless, but when that answer didn't satisfy her, Alex had grown irritated. I just do things sometimes, he'd said. It's no big deal.

Fool that she was then, it was much later before she finally connected Alex's impatience with the man they'd seen in the restaurant. He had watched them from a booth across the room, and Lissa couldn't help noting that he gave a sly grin every time she looked in his direction. When she'd mentioned him to Alex, he'd told her the guy was just some half-drunk jerk and to ignore him, but fifteen minutes later he'd hustled her out of the place. Even then, Lissa decided Alex was simply jealous of a strange man's attentions towards her.

It wasn't until after she'd learned of Alex's fiancée that Lissa realized the man must have been a friend of Alex's, someone who knew he was two-timing the woman he was to marry.

It was an unpleasant memory, as unpleasant as the time they'd run into Joe. Lissa could still see Joe's scowl, Alex's nervous discomfort a muted counterpoint to the disapproval etched on his brother's face.

She no longer harbored any feelings for Alex, other than sadness for the people he'd hurt, and, strangely, Joe no longer reminded her of Alex. He was stronger, more masculine, more demanding. And infinitely more dangerous.

Suzanne set up a babble of delighted commentary as Joe carried her inside the apartment, but Lissa was too tired to appreciate her daughter's chatter tonight. Just maintaining her composure in Joe's presence had taken all of her strength.

She took the baby from him, careful not to look into his face or let her fingers linger unduly on his hands. When she had changed her heavy-lidded baby into her sleeper and laid her in the alcove crib, she turned in the dusk of the room to find Joe standing behind her.

"Will she fall asleep all right?" he asked quietly.

Lissa nodded. "She's a good baby. She might wake in the middle of the night when her gums bother her, but she's happy most of the time."

Lissa walked past him, still not daring to look into his face.

She stood at the kitchen window, resting her hands on the cool wetness of the sink, thinking how hard it was to face Joe. She could stand the anger between them and the hostility, but she felt helpless in the face of her feelings whenever he touched her.

"She's asleep already," Joe said quietly from behind her, making her jump. "She's a beautiful child."

"Yes, she is." Lissa willed herself to look over her shoulder and meet his eyes. Tonight they were filled with shadows.

"Lissa, it's time we faced facts."

"Like the fact that you want to take my child from me," she said sharply. "And your first tactic is to move in across the hall. Do you think you'll be able to keep a better eye on me there? Is that it, Joe? Are you going to record each instance of my unfit parenting?"

"I'm not here to spy on you," he countered, tempted to take her in his arms and kiss her into silence—and maybe compliance. But he knew it would only be a temporary victory. Lissa would be even more determined to fight him if he reduced this to a physical confrontation. "I can help Mrs. McGee by fixing up the apartment," he said, trying to keep the impatience from his voice. "And I can be closer to help with Suzanne."

Frustration and a profound weariness pushed Lissa to near tears. "I don't want you here, Joe, and you know it."

He started to say something, then didn't, and they stared at each other until Lissa turned back to the window. She heard him give a weary sigh.

"At least take the damn hundred dollars," he said roughly.

"I don't want it," she insisted stubbornly.

"Lissa—" He broke off what he was going to say, and she could feel him struggling for control. "Take the money for the baby's sake. Alex would have wanted you to have it."

"For the baby's sake?" Lissa laughed shortly. "Do you really think Alex would have given a damn about the baby?" It was a harsh accusation, and Lissa heard Joe's sharp intake of breath. His hand closed on her shoulder, turning her to face him. Lissa's breath caught when she looked into his face. Anger and pain warred in his eyes.

"You didn't even care enough to tell any of us," he said. "You made the decision for everyone. It was you who judged my family and decided we weren't going to know about Suzanne."

His words made her wince, and Joe's arm abruptly fell from her shoulder.

"You don't know anything about this," she rasped furiously.

Joe's eyes narrowed. "I'll admit that Alex was selfish, yes, and self-centered. But, given half a chance, he would have loved his child. I'm his brother, Lissa. I'm the one who saw him play catch with my son until it was so dark out that neither one of them could see his hand in front of his face. And then Alex lay on his back on the ground and pointed out the stars to Jay. *That* was my brother, Lissa."

She didn't know when she'd started crying. But despite her determination not to let Joe make her cry she could feel the tears on her face. Before she could reach up a hand to brush them away, Joe gave a muttered oath and pulled her to him.

Lissa resisted at first, standing stiff and unyielding, but Joe's voice softened. "Don't cry," he said. "It's too late to change the past now."

His hand was smoothing her hair, and Lissa found her resolve weakening. With a groan that embodied the pain she'd held inside for so long, she let her head come to rest against Joe's broad chest, her hand curled under her chin.

"I'd be damned if I was going to ask any of your family for help," she whispered fiercely.

"I know," he said gently. "It doesn't matter now." But it did, and they both knew it.

Joe's hand reached to her cheek, gently brushing away a strand of hair caught in her tears. His fingers lingered, and she heard him groan from deep inside his chest. "Lissa . . ."

She looked up and saw her own need mirrored on Joe's face. They stared at each other a long moment, and Lissa knew that she was falling into a trap that was inescapable. This aching longing for Joe would bring her nothing but heartbreak. But still she didn't pull away from him.

She didn't protest when his mouth lowered to hers. Protest was futile when such need overwhelmed everything else. The first touch of his lips was electric. The ache inside her rose to meet the pleasure, colliding with explosive force. Lissa couldn't stop the groan that rose in her throat. Joe was right, the sexual energy between them was strong. It was a hot, bright force that overrode all her reserve. Lissa returned his kiss with an equal hunger, abandoning any pretense that she didn't want this.

"Joe . . ." she said when he raised his mouth to look at her, his eyes as turbulent as ever.

"What is it?" His voice was husky, and she could almost believe that he didn't hate her anymore.

"I can't handle this," she told him in all honesty.

He sighed roughly, smoothing back her hair again. "I know."

Lissa waited, feeling the tension inside him, the need to say something else.

"Hell," he swore softly, his thumb brushing away the last tear from her cheek. "We're a pair, aren't we? Nothing middle of the road since the minute we met. It's either open warfare or else we can't keep our hands off each other."

He forced himself to pull away from her, though it wrenched his gut to give up the soft feel of her and her sweet scent. "We need some ground rules here."

Lissa tilted up her chin and planted her hands on her hips. "The first one is that you don't try to touch me."

Joe shook his head. "No way I'm agreeing to that one," he said softly. "What I had in mind is that you stop trying to prevent me from getting to know Suzanne, and in return I'll make things a little easier for you."

"I can imagine what you mean by *a little easier*," she said sharply.

"Well, think again, sweetheart," he told her dryly. "When we go to bed, it'll be because you want it, too. And don't give me that outraged look. What I had in mind at the moment was more to do with finances. Here." He stepped toward her, controlling his irritation when he saw her brace herself. "Take the hundred dollars. We both know you need it, so stop playing these little games. You can buy something the baby needs." He pulled the money from his pocket and slapped it onto the counter. Lissa's shoulders stiffened, but at least she didn't throw it back in his face. He supposed that was progress. "Tomorrow I'll fix you something to eat after you get off work. That way you can get some studying done."

"Anything else?" she asked cheekily when he fell silent.

"Yeah," he said with a raise of his brows. "Wear that blouse again. I like it."

She flushed when she realized that with her arms spread, the blouse had tightened over her breasts, making them strain against the fabric.

"Only if you wear something for me," she retorted with mock sweetness.

"And what's that?" he said on his way to the door.

"A muzzle."

He didn't let her see his grim smile as he left.

Four

Sunday mornings at Duncans' Quik Shop had the blitz-krieg quality of a thundering cattle stampede.

Persons of varying and indeterminate age, weight, speed and sex, flowed nonstop through the door, wanting ice cream, donuts, newspapers, soda, gas for their cars and cough drops for their children. They came with perky smiles, martyrs' forebearance, surly frowns, frayed tempers, killer hangovers and troubles counting out money.

In short, it was a zoo.

"Where is this tidal wave of humanity coming from?" Bonnie Ann wailed after two older women on their way to church exited, carrying two banana splits that Lissa could only hope they weren't planning on devouring inside the sanctuary.

"It's Sunday, Bonnie Ann," Lissa reminded her with a light tap on top of her friend's unruly hair. "Our busy day. Remember?"

Lissa was glad of the extra business, because it took her mind off her encounter with Joe Douglas the night before. She kept hearing him telling her that when he took her to bed, she would want it as much as he did. She would have liked to have thrown his words back in his teeth, but she would be lying. She'd lived her life at a breakneck pace since the baby was born, hours of work and study to keep busy and make ends meet. Her mind may have forgotten what it was like to be with a man, but her body remembered well enough to ache for Joe's seduction.

The next customer pulled Lissa back to the present, and she relegated Joe to that walled-off recess of her mind where he couldn't touch her. When she'd checked out the last customer fifteen minutes later, she raised her head to see a serious, dark-haired boy studying her from in front of the counter.

"Hi," Lissa said. "Can I help you with something?"

The boy pondered that a moment. "I guess so," he said. "I'm looking for those...those cars. You know, the ones you get with the candy bar."

"Ah, I know just what you mean." Lissa came around the counter and put her arm on his shoulder, steering him to a display hanging in the candy aisle. "Are you in the market for a four-door or something more sporty, say the Jaguar here?" She pointed to a red plastic car packaged with a large candy bar and raised her brows to show she was impressed with his taste.

The boy grinned. "Yeah, the Jag," he said. "My favorite. The candy bar's pretty good, too," he advised her wisely as he took down the plastic case and inspected it. Lissa smiled back, judging him to be about ten and long on cute. Most often, the young boys who came into the store were running errands for their parents, picking up jugs of milk or liters of soda for someone waiting in the car. They seldom shopped for themselves.

"You find what you wanted?" a familiar voice asked, and Lissa looked up in surprise to see Joe watching the boy. She looked back down and saw the resemblance suddenly. This was Joe's son.

"Yeah, I found the Jag," the boy said, holding up the plastic.

"Nice car," Joe said approvingly. His voice when he addressed his son was warm and affectionate, without a trace of the sardonic edge Lissa had heard so often. His eyes drifted up to Lissa's, and he cleared his throat. "Jay, this is the lady I was telling you about, Lissa Gray. Lissa, this is my son Jay."

Jay looked at her with renewed interest, his dark eyes so like his father's. "She knows cars," he assured his dad, who smiled. His son certainly made Joe more relaxed, she decided.

"I didn't know Jay was in town," she said.

"I drove over to my mother's and picked him up early this morning," Joe said, stepping out of the way of a heavy woman laden with donuts and ice cream. "Missouri schools let out last Friday, and he had his class picnic yesterday."

"Grandma took me because Mom was in one of her moods," Jay said, and the adult note of pain in his voice made Lissa look quickly at Joe. But Joe's eyes were unreadable.

"Is she going with us?" Jay asked his father.

"I don't know," Joe said. "We haven't asked her, have we?"

"I guess not," Jay agreed.

"Do you think maybe you could do that?" Joe asked the boy.

"Yeah, I guess," Jay said shyly after pondering a moment.

Lissa waited, not sure at all what they had in mind. She was still reeling from meeting Joe's son.

"We're going up to the lake," Jay said. "You want to come along?"

"You want to come along?" Joe repeated. "Now there's an elegant invitation."

"Well, geez, Dad," the boy protested. "What am I supposed to say?"

"How about 'Miss Lissa, would you care to accompany us gentlemen to Marshall Lake for an afternoon of frolicking and general amusement?'" Joe said in a deadpan Southern drawl. Jay laughed. "Haven't I taught you anything about impressing the ladies?" Joe ribbed him.

"Yeah, you told me not to spit or belch or let any other air escape my body when I'm around them," Jay said, rolling his eyes in apparent embarrassment at his father's pitiful knowledge of women. Lissa suppressed a smile. Joe was a different person around his son, and the change dazzled her.

"How rewarding for your old dad to have you remember that particular piece of advice," Joe said ruefully, thumping Jay lightly on the head.

"Hey, I'm *ten,*" Jay said pointedly. "I don't forget stuff like little kids do."

"Yeah, I keep forgetting," Joe said. "You're getting to be a regular old man. Now, what do you say we two old men ask Lissa real nice if she'd go with us?"

Lissa broke in, enjoying their banter but not wanting to lead them on. "I appreciate the invitation, but I really can't," she said.

"I promised I'd fix you something to eat today," Joe reminded her.

"I have to work until noon," Lissa said. "And then I have to study for a test. And Mrs. McGee can't watch the baby this afternoon."

"No problem," Joe assured her. "We can leave after you get off work and we'll take Suzanne with us. And bring your books to study. We'll help, won't we, Jay?"

Jay nodded his head. "I know all about studying," he informed her.

Still Lissa hesitated. She didn't know if Jay would pick up on the undercurrents between her and Joe, and if he did, how he would react to them.

"Listen," Jay said, apparently resorting to bald-faced honesty, if his expression was any indication. "My dad is just about the weirdest cook in the world. I mean it. He fixes junk that no one would eat. He won't fix anything normal like hot dogs. *Hot dogs,*" Jay repeated in outrage. "If you don't come, I don't know what will happen to my stomach."

"Heaven knows I can't have your stomach on my conscience," Lissa said, giving in. Joe had already made it plain that she should take seriously his threat to gain custody of her baby if she didn't let him spend time with Suzanne. Lissa decided that if she granted him the time, then maybe he would back off. What surprised her was that Jay actually seemed to want her to come along, as well, and it made her wonder even more about the look on his face when he'd mentioned his mother.

"Your cooking must be *really* bad," she said to Joe as she headed back to the counter, with him in her wake.

"Just the opposite," he said dryly, leaning a muscular forearm on the counter as she took up her position behind the register. "I can outchef a Cordon Bleu graduate any day of the week."

At her look of surprise, he said, "My mother's French. Dad was in the army. He was stationed in Germany when she came there on holiday with her parents. They got married when he was sent back to the States. One of the many things Mom taught me was how to cook."

"But Jay said—" she began in confusion.

"The problem is that I have a kid who hates cassoulet and vichyssoise," he said, raising an eyebrow. "Hence, I'd better stock up on potato chips and hot dogs." Shaking his head, he ambled off.

Lissa stared after him, confounded. When she'd finished ringing up three frozen pizzas for two giggling teenage girls, she saw Jay standing by the counter with his toy car, his eyes on his dad who was still browsing in the snacks aisle.

His eyes were worried when he looked up at Lissa. The boy sighed. "He looks tired, doesn't he?" Without waiting for her answer, he went on. "Sometimes he has trouble sleeping. Especially after my mother calls him. I told him nothing would happen to me, but I guess that's just how dads are."

Lissa felt all the weight of the ten-year-old's concern for his dad, and she wondered again what had happened between Joe and his ex-wife. Whatever the circumstances of Joe's divorce, it had certainly been painful enough to cause man and boy to worry about each other.

When Joe came back with the potato chips and hot dogs, she realized that he did indeed look tired. His face was all hard angles and underneath that a haunted tautness. "We'll pick you up at your apartment, at twelve-thirty, and pack a swimsuit," he said, his eyes on her as she rang up his purchase. She could feel her body heating under his gaze, and her fingers were suddenly clumsy at their task. She managed to hand him his change, her hand coming close to trembling when their fingers brushed.

He moved aside for another customer, pocketing his wallet and giving her a last, lingering glance before going out the door. Lissa was left staring after him, her heart still pounding against her ribs.

"Malts coming through!" Bonnie Ann announced, her hips bumping Lissa to the side as she maneuvered behind the counter. "Everybody inhale!"

The malts safely delivered and the sale rung up, Bonnie Ann lowered her head near Lissa's on her way back to the front counter. "Did I hear you make a date with Joe?"

"It's nothing," Lissa told her as she counted out change for a woman who'd just bought two gallons of ice cream and a six-pack of diet soda. "Just a picnic at the lake." She frowned. "I really can't deny him the right to see Suzanne." She'd already told Bonnie Ann that Joe was Suzanne's uncle, recognizing that Bonnie Ann would dog her unmercifully until she got the information she wanted.

"Was that his kid in here with him? Cute little son-of-a-gun."

"Uh-huh." Lissa pretended to study the sale price on a half gallon of mint chip ice cream. She was still puzzling over Jay's remark about his mother, and she didn't want to bring Bonnie Ann, with her finely honed curiosity, into the matter. The woman could have been an ace reporter for the *Washington Post* if she'd been so inclined. As it was, she directed her hyperactivity into other diversions—cooking, sewing, organizing and relentlessly pursuing rumors large and small.

"You know," Bonnie Ann began with that narrow-eyed tunnel-vision expression Lissa had come to recognize and dread, "I've been trying to remember something I heard several years ago about someone whose last name was Douglas. You know my cousin Sherry who lives near Pittman? I could ask her."

Lissa shook her head. She'd decided to be adult about this and not pursue rumors about Joe, no matter how badly she really wanted to know.

"It had something to do with a child custody case," Bonnie Ann went on, apparently oblivious to Lissa's refusal. And despite her good intentions, Lissa couldn't forget Jay's face. Adult or not, suddenly her curiosity was piqued.

"All right," she acquiesced, trying to ignore her own guilt about her nosiness. "Next time you talk to Sherry, ask her."

Lissa and the baby were packed and ready to go when Joe and Jay picked them up at the apartment. She was surprised when he opened the door to a late-model red sports car, especially when she saw his pickup truck parked behind the car. But Joe didn't say a word about their mode of transportation, and she didn't ask any questions. She settled the baby in her car seat in the half-back seat with her favorite green plush toy, a frog, and Jay climbed in beside her. Joe held the passenger door for Lissa, blatantly eyeing the length of satiny leg that her shorts exposed. When her eyes met his, he smiled. "I think I like those shorts even better than the pink blouse." His eyes gleamed wickedly. "I couldn't find my muzzle this morning," he said with a raise of his dark brows just before he closed the door.

Lissa held her smile as he slid into the seat next to her. He had caught her off guard, teasing her when she'd least expected it. It seemed that Joe could be charming when he wanted, and apparently today was one of those times.

Jay chattered most of the way, filling in Lissa on his school and his friends, though he didn't mention his mother again.

"So, do you come here often?" Joe said conversationally as they got out of the car, which had been parked in the gravel lot at the lake. He and Jay began unloading a picnic basket from the back while Lissa got the baby.

"No," Lissa said. "I've never been here."

"Never been here?" Joe asked incredulously.

Lissa shrugged. "I don't have much time to get out, what with the baby and my schedule."

"I intend to remedy that," Joe pronounced. He nudged Jay with his elbow and grinned. "We've got a new one for the water slide," he said in an undertone.

"Why does that sound ominous?" she asked as both males worked hard at looking innocent.

"You're in for a treat," was all Joe would say.

"This water slide," Lissa ventured when Joe had claimed a picnic table under the shade trees and was depositing their supplies onto it. "Is it very high?"

"Like Niagara Falls," Joe assured her, his lips twitching slightly.

"I see. Should I take out additional insurance or anything like that?"

"They have one of those machines that sells insurance by the slide," he teased her. "Just like the airport."

"How reassuring," she murmured, enjoying the way Joe and his son exchanged conspiratorial grins again. It was the kind of relationship she wanted to develop with Suzanne.

"The slide beckons," Joe said. "Are you game?" He was unfastening his jeans and kicking off his sneakers, and for a moment Lissa was arrested by the sight of his hard, muscled legs with their dark hair. At least he hadn't worn one of those brief swimsuits that was so flimsy it was more like a snood than something to swim in. Still, his black trunks afforded her a breathtaking view of his long thighs. Forcing her eyes upward, she focused on the oversized wristwatch he was wearing. Then, steeling herself, she turned away and began stripping off her own clothes.

When she turned back in her two-piece red suit, the only swimsuit she owned, Joe was watching her appreciatively and unabashedly.

"You look...nice," he said.

His eyes were saying a lot more than *nice*, and it made her bare skin tingle as though he were caressing her. He'd taken off his shirt, and his chest was like the rest of his body, hard and muscled and incredibly inviting. The hair there was darker and thicker.

"So," she said to take her mind off her quickening pulse. "Does Dick Tracy know you've got his watch?"

"Very funny, Lissa," he said, but he was smiling. "This is Jay's. He ordered it from the back of one of those cereal boxes. I used to have a working watch of my own." He raised his brows significantly. "That's past tense."

"Mrs. McGee strikes again," Lissa murmured, trying to sound sympathetic and not grin too much. "How fast does it run now?"

He shook his head. "It's slow now, not fast. Loses at least two hours a day. I don't know how Mrs. McGee does it."

"It's a gift," Lissa told him dryly. "All right." She hoisted the baby from the blanket. "Now where's this slide?"

"She sure does look nice, doesn't she?" Joe remarked again, this time to Jay, as they walked from the trees toward the water slide at the top of the hill to their right.

Jay grinned at his father. "Yeah, Dad. She sure does."

The lake stretched out blue and placid before them, the sun glinting off it like glass. A group of children frolicked in the roped-off swimming area, splashing around the lifeguard's tower. Farther out, where the lake made a lazy turn by a sandy beach, a few sailboats tested what breeze there was. There were a lot of people here today, but the lake was so large and so winding, that they were well distributed, and no one place was crowded.

They climbed to the top of the hill, and Joe paid for a ride for the two of them. "You watch the baby, okay?" he said to Jay, and Jay took her from Lissa.

"You think she's a screamer, Dad?" Jay asked, his eyes dancing as he teased Lissa.

"Naw," Joe said, appraising Lissa. "More of a shrieker, I'd say."

Lissa didn't mention that she liked water slides. She figured that was something these two arrogant males didn't need to know at the moment.

She picked up one of the rubber mats to sit on and looked around to see that Joe was right behind her but with no mat. She gave him a quizzical look when he took the mat from her.

"It's your first trip and all," he said. "So I thought we'd go down together."

"Did you come up with this idea all by yourself?"

"Yeah." He grinned at her. "It's a gift."

Lissa murmured something noncommittal and watched him drop the mat and sit. He patted the space in front of him. "All aboard!"

He was being just too cute for words, and he knew it. But Lissa couldn't resist him. She gave him a resigned look and sat down in front of him. "Long way down, isn't it?" she said with relish as she glanced over the edge of the slide. It felt like years since she'd done anything for the pure fun of it. Now with the light breeze playing around her hair and the water stretching out invitingly below, she could swear she was light-years away from her everyday problems.

"Have you done this before?" Joe demanded suspiciously.

"Who, me?"

"Yeah. You." He settled his long legs on the outside of hers and wrapped his arms around her waist. "By the way, did I tell you you look good in that swimsuit?"

"No!" she said, a bit embarrassed. But she couldn't help smiling when he gave her an exasperated look, and then he shoved off down the slide. Lissa wasn't sure what was affecting her more, the exhilarating speed or Joe's arms around her. Whichever it was, her blood was singing. As the mat slid over the first small rise, Lissa lifted her arms in the air and tilted her head back until it almost touched Joe's shoulder. Closing her eyes, she let the wind rush over her. They sailed over another rise, making Joe slide forward even closer. Lissa could feel his springy chest hair tickling her back and his breath on her neck.

She was really enjoying this. Joe could hardly take his eyes off her, which was why he was disoriented and felt his stomach fly into the air each time they topped a rise. She was so pretty and sassy that it was all he could do not to kiss her right in front of Jay. Not that Jay would mind. His kid was always telling him that he needed some romance in his life.

Most kids of divorced parents fed on the fantasy that their parents would get back together somehow, but not Jay. Having seen his mother's life-style firsthand, he was too much of a realist. Joe couldn't blame him, but he felt sorry for what his son had gone through.

Lissa's hair brushed his cheek as they flew down the slide, the fresh, clean scent filling Joe's nostrils. He liked the way she smelled and the way she teased him back and smiled. It was becoming harder for him to hold his image of her as the callous, conniving bitch who'd caused so much damage. When she smiled, she didn't seem capable of anything so coldhearted. He had to keep reminding himself that looks were deceiving.

They shot down the last incline faster and hung a moment suspended in air before dropping into the water. Both went under, arms and legs tangled, and Lissa surfaced first, flushed and laughing.

"It's cold!" she exclaimed, her laughter echoing across the water as he came up beside her, his hands automatically going to her arms as she temporarily lost her balance when another slider entered the water near them with a shriek.

Joe was mesmerized by the sound. He hadn't heard her laugh like that before, and now it fueled his never diminishing need to touch her. His hands tightened on her arms, his thumbs stroking softly, and her laughter caught in her throat. She stared back at him, seeing raw need in his eyes and knowing her face mirrored the same. Pink colored her cheeks, and then she turned her head, making a pretense of searching for the mat. Joe slowly released her.

They climbed up the stairs at the side, Joe carrying the mat, Lissa still feeling the touch of his body against hers, as though he'd just made love to her. He was a complicated man, and she still couldn't begin to understand him.

He had been cold and ruthless when she'd first met him, and yet he was gentle and loving with his son, and he was taking pains to make her have a good time. She didn't know what had changed, other than his confession that he wanted her. Certainly his opinion of her hadn't. Every now and then, she caught the wariness in his eyes, the shadowy look that spoke volumes about his mistrust for her. It was right there, coexisting with the desire.

"Gosh, you didn't even scream," Jay said in admiration when they reached the top. "And you went down with your arms up in the air. That's like something Arnold Schwartzenegger would do."

Lissa realized that that was high praise indeed from a ten-year-old boy.

"Only you're prettier," Jay amended, and Lissa laughed.

Lissa held the baby while Jay took his turn on the slide. "Man, I'm starved!" he proclaimed when he reached the top again. "Dad, did you bring any decent food?"

"Of course I did," Joe said, clearly offended by his son's assessment of his shopping abilities. "I brought potato chips and hot dogs and brownies for you."

"Really?" Jay said suspiciously. "What was that other junk I saw you packing?"

Joe rolled his eyes. "Decent food for Lissa and me. Don't worry—I'm not going to force-feed you anything."

Jay grinned and danced away from his father's arm that was about to snare him in a mock neckhold. "Come on!" he said. "I'm starved."

Lissa laid Suzanne down on the blanket, then wrapped her beach towel around her waist and helped Joe cook on the barbecue grill near their picnic table. Jay was hovering nearby giving advice. "Dad, don't turn that hot dog," Jay warned. "I like them crisp."

"Thank you, Julia Child," Joe grumbled good-naturedly.

"Yuck!" Jay said when he saw what his father was setting on the table.

Lissa watched in wide-eyed amazement. "You made this?" she said, staring at the long loaf of bread, the plate of pâté and the cold sliced meat and cheese.

"I hope my culinary skills are impressing you," Joe said to Lissa as he broke off a chunk of bread, spread some pâté on it and popped it into her mouth.

"More than you know," she told him truthfully. "This beats the heck out of macaroni and cheese."

She fed Suzanne applesauce and cereal while Joe fixed a plate of food for her, the baby signaling her approval by flailing her arms up and down. Lissa ate with gusto. The meat tasted of a piquant marinade and went perfectly with the cheese and bread. When she thought she couldn't eat another bite, Joe surprised her with a wonderful apple flan. She couldn't remember when she'd had such a good meal and she told him so. The smile he gave her set her blood racing all over again.

Afterward, Joe and Lissa lay on a blanket on the ground in the shade while Jay went down the slide. The baby lay dozing in her infant carrier next to Joe. It surprised Lissa that she could enjoy herself so much with Joe. She felt totally relaxed and sated.

She glanced over at him and saw that his eyes were closed. He'd pulled on his shirt and lay on his back, one leg bent and his hands laced behind his head.

"You're supposed to be studying," he said without opening his eyes.

Lissa tentatively waved a hand in front of his face, but he didn't budge. "So, you have X-ray vision?" she said.

"Nope." Joe grinned, still without opening his eyes. "I have a ten-year-old kid," he informed her. "I can *feel* these things going on. Like vibrations. And I don't feel any school books being opened. It's a gift," he added.

"Sure," Lissa agreed. "Right up there with your cooking gift."

He grinned again, and Lissa studied him absently while she sat up and settled her English lit book on her lap. His good looks were really breathtaking. A few flecks of sun rays, drifting like smoke through the canopy of green leaves above, highlighted his hair with golden sparks. His skin was already bronzed from his outdoor work, giving even more definition to the hard muscles beneath. There was an edge of weariness around his eyes, a tension at the mouth. She wondered idly if she was the cause or if it had something to do with his ex-wife.

Stealing one last look at his face, she opened her book to William Blake and tried to concentrate on the words in the "Songs of Experience." She got through the poems about the chimney-sweeper child and about what the poet saw on the streets of London. But her mind stumbled over a poem about love. The man in the poem frightened away the woman with his deep protestations of love, while a stranger won her with no more than a sigh.

An empty-headed woman who capitulated to a man she didn't know over nothing more than a sigh. It was a weakness that Lissa could understand. Every smile or small kindness that Joe gave her only weakened her resolve further. He was the man who threatened to take her child from her, the man who mistrusted and judged her. And yet...

And yet he was the man who'd awakened feelings she hadn't known before, whose touch could dissolve her bones. She wanted to run from him. She wanted to run so far that Joe couldn't even guess which country was harboring her. But she knew deep down that she wouldn't run from him. The past had taught her one thing, she was through with fleeing her troubles.

"What are you reading?" he asked suddenly, his eyes opening, and she started guiltily, as though he'd walked into her reverie and heard it all.

"Poetry," she said, managing to pull her eyes from his face and back to the book. "William Blake."

"Read to me," he said, shifting so he was leaning on his elbow. "It's been a long time since I heard any poetry."

Lissa made a face. "You don't want to hear this."

"Yeah, I do. Besides, I like to hear your voice."

That set her back a bit, and she studied him a moment before letting her eyes drop back to the book. He wasn't teasing her. Apparently he really did want to hear her read William Blake out loud. Which unnerved her even more.

Lissa frowned over the book, looking for something appropriate. She settled on a poem about a fly and read that, her voice wavering a bit at first, then growing stronger.

Joe was quiet a moment, and she could feel his eyes on her as he asked her to read another one. She started a new poem, one about a chunk of dirt and a pebble, but she faltered on the first line when she realized it was about love, about two uniquely opposite ways of seeing it.

"Go on," Joe prompted her.

Lissa cleared her throat and read the rest, falling quiet when she was done.

The silence hung between them, as though suspended on the early-summer air. When she dared a glance at Joe, she saw that he was staring down at the blanket, the lines at his eyes and mouth etched deeper. Love hadn't been kind to either of them, she thought.

"Mr. Blake knew a lot about love," he said at last. "It's either heaven or hell."

"Sometimes it's something in between," she said. "Sometimes it's just…something you don't think about or talk about." It was the way she'd felt about her mother, not even daring to wonder how her mother felt about her, how she could leave her with her grandmother.

"That's indifference, Lissa," Joe countered. "Love's dead then."

"No," she said, refusing to believe it. "I don't buy that." She'd hooked her arms around her knees and now she rested her chin there.

"What do you buy?" Joe asked, and she could feel his eyes on her. "Love is eternal? Is that what you believe?" There was skepticism in his voice and the slightest hint of a taunt.

"It *should* be," she insisted fiercely, turning her head to look at him. "It should be the best thing this world has to offer. And when it's right, then it *is* the best thing." She spoke almost desperately, out of a need to convince herself, because it never had been that right for her, unless she counted her love for Suzanne. But she'd never loved a man like that. Love had never mattered over everything else, and it had never been the best thing in the world.

She really wanted to believe that, Joe thought, watching the light chase over her eyes. She wanted the white lace and promises in the song or at the least some guarantee that they really existed somewhere. There was a child's hunger in those blue eyes. He wondered if that need had driven her into the arms of other men before his brother. To his surprise, he felt a stab of jealousy. He didn't want other men to have touched her; he didn't want her to have felt anything for them, even for his own brother.

Lissa saw censure in the eyes that starkly appraised her.

"Even when love starts out right, it can lead you straight to hell," he said evenly. "That's a hard lesson to learn, but the world would be better off if more people learned it. It would save a lot of grief." Lissa saw his eyes drift toward the water slide and Jay. "It would save a lot of grief for the innocents, too."

There was more than a little rancor—and pain—in his voice.

"You don't believe in love then?" she asked.

"Let's just say I don't have a lot of faith in it. It seems one partner always succumbs to the temptation to take advantage of the other."

She looked away, feeling that his words may have been his assessment of her.

"Why haven't you ever been here?" he asked, abruptly changing the subject.

Lissa gave him an incredulous look as her hands indicated her lit book and the baby. "I told you. I just don't have the time."

Joe shrugged. "You could always bring Suzanne and study here." His eyes were relentless. "Why do you bury yourself in work?"

Lissa stared at him, not knowing what to say. Didn't he understand that she couldn't let herself have fun now? She had too much at stake. Suzanne was her joy; she lived for her, and she wouldn't let her daughter get hurt. She wouldn't let her own heart be hurt again, either.

"What are you afraid of?" he demanded.

She worked to keep her composure, combing through her jumbled thoughts for a measured reply until Jay's voice cut through her tension.

"Hey, you guys! You going down the slide again?"

Joe stared at Lissa a moment longer before he turned to his son, mustering a smile. "Aren't you waterlogged yet?"

"Daa-ad," Jay protested, but the corners of his mouth inched up in a smile. "Come on, you guys. You're wasting a whole lake."

Joe stood and looked expectantly at Lissa, but she waved him off. "You go on and have fun with Jay. I've got studying to do." Resolutely bending her head to her book, she didn't look up again until the two had moved away. Then she couldn't seem to stop looking at them. Father and son. So like each other. Jay was going to be as handsome as his father. Their dark heads close together, they were settling on mats at the top of the slide, joking with each other and laughing. Lissa watched them, her heart breaking. The man was so lonely, the boy so worried about his dad. And she was feeling things she shouldn't, emotions that had no place in her life. But maybe that was what he wanted. He'd already reproached her; maybe bedding her was what he considered fitting punishment. She almost shivered when she thought of the worst he could do—follow through on his threat to take away Suzanne. Absently she watched the two disappear from sight down the slide, her fingers pressing at the incipient headache at her temple.

The air was even more humid when they left the lake late that afternoon, and the sun slanted sharply through the windshield, intensifying Lissa's headache. The baby was uncomfortable and fussy, and Lissa had to keep shifting around to comfort her. Jay, exhausted from the sun and water, fell asleep in the little back seat. Joe shot Lissa dozens of sideways glances but didn't speak.

Jay awoke briefly when Joe stopped the car in front of Lissa's house. He roused himself enough to give Lissa a sleepy grin and tell her he'd had a great time. And she'd looked great in her swimsuit, he added.

"That's the way to do it, son," Joe praised him, ruffling his hair.

Balancing the baby, Lissa reached for the diaper bag in the back, but Joe swung it up before she could get it. She could see that he had something on his mind as she led the way to the back of the house. "Thanks for the afternoon," she said, picking up two clothespins and pinning her swimsuit to the line.

"Here," he said, and as she turned he took her wrist and dropped the car keys onto her palm.

"What's this?" she said, frowning.

"I want you to take the car," he said. "I don't want you driving that rattletrap of yours." He jerked his head derisively toward her car sitting in the gravel lot.

"I can't take your car," she said incredulously.

"Yes, you can," he insisted. "I'm surprised you even got yours past the state inspection. What did you do, wear those shorts?"

She didn't tell him that she owed that miracle to another of Bonnie Ann's cousins who'd patched the car into somewhat acceptable shape before the inspection. Instead, she fixed him with an icy glare.

"All right, sorry," he said, shrugging. "I didn't mean that."

"Like hell you didn't."

"Look, I just don't want you sliding through some red light when your brakes fail." He was still holding her wrist, effectively preventing her from throwing the car keys back at him.

"Why should you care about my car?" she demanded, her temper flaring at his high-handed manner. "You can't just come around and bully me into doing whatever you want."

"If that's what it takes, I will," he assured her. "I told you before, I'm going to make sure you take good care of the baby, and if part of that bargain means making sure you drive a safe car, then that's the way it's going to be."

Lissa raised her chin fractionally. "And if I don't drive your car or I don't use your diaper service, what then? Is that grounds enough for you to take Suzanne? I don't want you running my life, Joe!"

"Dammit, Lissa! Listen to reason. I'm only trying to help you, but if you persist in being so obstinate, you'll find out you can't dump me as easily as you did my brother."

His grip had tightened on her wrist, and her fingers curled in white-hot anger. "I didn't dump your brother, so you can stop throwing that up at me."

"And what would you call it?" he snapped. "You got tired of him and left. Technically, that's dumping, sweetheart."

The taunt snapped something inside Lissa.

Her voice was shaking with fury when she answered him. "I want one thing straight between us, Joe," she said. "I didn't dump Alex, whatever you think. I left when I found out he was engaged to someone else."

His look of shock should have rendered her silent, but the angry words kept spilling out.

"I didn't care what you thought when you first came to see me. In fact, I thought you were just like your brother— selfish and callous. Well, maybe you're not like Alex. But I'm still not going to let you run my life."

Joe stood stock-still, his eyes riveted to Lissa's face, and she felt the first wave of revulsion at what she'd said. "I don't care anymore what he did," she said. "I just don't care. You don't have to do anything for the baby and me. You don't have to fix up Mrs. McGee's apartment. You don't have to worry about my car." She could feel the tears welling up in her eyes, and the baby began to grow restless.

"You didn't know he was engaged?" he demanded incredulously, and she could see that he didn't believe her. "How could you not know? Everybody in town knew."

"So why didn't one of those upright citizens tell me?" she countered. "Why did Alex only take me to out-of-the-way places where I wouldn't meet anyone he knew? Why did he hustle me away after we ran into you that time? Why, Joe?"

"You couldn't *not* have known," he said, still incredulous.

"The hell I couldn't," she snapped, pulling her wrist from his grasp, acutely aware of the lingering sensation of his touch.

A sound made them both turn, and Lissa's heart clutched when she saw Jay standing at the corner of the house, watching them, his eyes wide. "Suzanne's toy," he said lamely, holding up the green cloth frog. "I...found it on the floor." He slowly walked toward them, looking from one to the other as if for reassurance, and dropped the toy on top of the diaper bag.

"Come on, Jay," Joe said gently, putting his arm around the boy's shoulders. "Let's go."

Jay was still staring up at his father's face, worriedly trying to decipher what he saw there as they walked away.

"Oh, damn," Lissa murmured, jiggling Suzanne as the baby began to cry. Slowly she opened her fist, realizing she'd been clutching the keys so tightly that there was a ridged imprint of them on her palm.

Five

It was seven o'clock and Joe hadn't touched the open can of beer on the desk in front of him since he'd popped the tab an hour ago. Water had condensed on the side and now pooled on the desk's glass surface. Absently, he ran his thumb over the can's lip and then stared straight ahead at his reflection in the motel mirror.

The eyes staring back were haunted with misery, and all too familiar. He'd seen himself every time he'd looked at Alex's eyes, the one feature they'd shared. His own gaze was still a grim reminder of his brother when he caught himself unawares in a mirror.

His brother had had no talent for happiness. And Joe had begun to believe that neither did he. He'd never found what he wanted or needed and his ex-wife certainly hadn't, either. One time Joe thought that Alex had finally done it; he was engaged to a nice woman and he seemed genuinely happy. But that was before Joe saw his brother with Lissa Gray. He knew then that Alex had lost his chance.

And Joe had blamed Lissa for that. She'd ruined Alex's chance, his last chance as it turned out.

Behind him, Jay stirred in the bed. "Dad?" he said sleepily. "When are you coming to bed?"

"In a little bit, son," Joe said quietly. Without moving his eyes from the mirror, he reached over and switched off the dim light hanging from the ceiling. There was never enough light in a motel room to suit Joe, but that was a blessing tonight with Jay trying to sleep.

There wouldn't be any sleep for Joe, no matter when he went to bed. What Lissa had told him in anger today kept echoing in his head. *She hadn't known that Alex was engaged. She hadn't known.* He lowered his head and rested his forehead on the heels of his hands. How could she not have known? he demanded.

She had said that Alex kept her away from friends and family, from anyone else who knew he was engaged. That was possible, but to believe that, he had to believe that Alex was capable of deceiving two women at the same time. And betraying them both.

Joe knew his brother better than anyone—or at least he had always thought he did—and now he weighed what he knew. Alex was selfish, but at the same time he could be generous with his family. He had never sustained a lasting relationship with a woman, and it was always Alex who ended it, at least until Lissa. And he openly bragged about his women and showed them off. Until Lissa. He had to admit that she was right about that. Alex had taken great pains to keep her away from his family.

Joe could still remember the night he ran into Alex and Lissa as though it were yesterday. She was so pretty, and her smile had seemed so calculating. Even then and against his will, Joe was drawn to her. Alex had explained her away later, claiming she was a friend of a friend, someone he'd run into at a bar and who had attached herself to him. He was trying to shake her off, he'd said.

Clearly Alex had lied.

Joe rubbed his hands over his eyes. It was so damn hard trying to sort out the truth where Alex was concerned. From the time they were children, Alex had twisted the truth to keep himself out of trouble. The sad fact was that Alex actually believed his own version of it, no matter what the contradictory evidence. He was so convincing that Joe had gotten himself in trouble time and again sticking up for his younger brother when Alex got in some scrape. Alex was a charmer, and people wanted to believe him.

Especially Joe. He'd always believed that deep down Alex was an honorable man, that his mistakes were only that— mistakes.

And now he was faced with the possibility that one of those mistakes might have been something more. Was Alex capable of that kind of deception? Or was Lissa lying to save face?

Lissa was bone-tired when she got out of class Tuesday afternoon, but Suzanne's cheerful babbling made her smile as she carried her inside the apartment. Dropping her books on the table, she set the baby and her infant carrier on the table and tickled her lightly under the chin.

"Mrs. McGee says you ate all your strained beef tonight, Hot Stuff," she cooed as Suzanne grinned and kicked. "Aren't you the clever baby?"

A loud bang at the back door startled Lissa, and she stroked the baby's head as Suzanne's eyes widened. "Hold on," Lissa whispered. "Let your old mom investigate."

Lissa tiptoed to the door and opened it a crack, peering out into the darkened hall. She could hear muffled cursing at the foot of the stairs and then a familiar voice. "Jeez,

Dad,'' Jay complained. "The light switch is right here.''
Lissa quietly withdrew and shut the door as light suddenly
pooled in the hall.

She couldn't forget the image of Joe's face two days ago
when she'd told him the truth about his brother and her. The
shock and accusation in his eyes had haunted her sleep. And
she'd come to the hard realization that it did matter to her
what Joe thought of her.

Yesterday, she'd seen the man from the electric company
here, so it wasn't entirely a surprise to see Joe moving in.
Nevertheless, she jumped when someone knocked on the
door, swiftly checking the jeans and pink shell she wore before answering.

It was Jay. He looked furtively down the stairs, and Lissa
guessed that his father didn't know he was knocking on her
door.

"We're moving in,'' he said hesitantly. "And I was wondering...well, it's kind of hot and...you wouldn't have any
soda, would you?''

Lissa smiled at him. "Why don't we see what's in the refrigerator?'' Jay looked tremendously relieved, and Lissa
felt guilty for letting him see her fight with his father on
Sunday. Apparently, the boy had witnessed more than
enough hostility between Joe and his ex-wife.

Jay drank his soda, chattering to her about the movie he'd
seen on TV the night before. He held out his finger for Suzanne to clutch, then grinned and headed for the door.
"Listen,'' he said. "We want you and Suzie to come over for
dinner after we're all done unpacking.''

Lissa's eyebrows shot up. "We who?''

"Me and Dad,'' he said, his grin broadening.

"Jay,'' she said, worried about his high expectations for
her and Joe. "Your dad and I aren't getting along the best
right now. Maybe you ought to talk to him before you issue
any invitations.''

"Nah," Jay assured her. "I know Dad. He'll come around."

Lissa wasn't so sure of that, but Jay apparently harbored no doubts. He peeked into the hall—to establish his father's whereabouts, she decided—then slipped out the door.

He was back ten minutes later to use the bathroom and to ask if she was busy later that evening.

"Jay, I really don't think—" she began, but he wouldn't be deterred.

"Dad said we were going to order out pizza tonight. I only eat three pieces, so there'll be plenty for you. You don't like green peppers, do you?" he asked as that horrible possibility struck him.

"I can take them or leave them," she assured him. "But, Jay—"

"Gotta go."

He was gone again, only to reappear fifteen minutes later, hungry and wondering if she had any cookies. And again he issued his dinner invitation, this time accompanied by a request that she provide the dessert, assuring her that cookies would do just fine.

There were bumping sounds coming from the stairs and then Joe's voice hollering Jay's name.

"Oops," Jay said, looking guilty. "He told me not to bother you." Shrugging philosophically, he opened the door. "You wanted me, Dad?"

"Yeah." Past Jay, Lissa could see Joe, looking tired and sweaty, a folding cot resting on the landing. "I need you to help me get us moved in. And what did I tell you about bothering people?"

"Don't go knocking on other people's doors," Jay repeated dutifully if a little impatiently.

"Right. Now come on." Joe reached an arm around Jay's shoulder and pulled him outside. For just an instant, he let himself look at Lissa, and she thought she saw a flash of some emotion in his eyes, something raw and sensual. But the landing was dim, and she couldn't be sure. Her heart pounded faster anyway.

She could hear them from time to time, their voices mingling as they crested the top of the stairs with yet another load. About two hours later, while she was rocking the baby and reading her history assignment, she heard muffled voices outside her door. Apparently there was some kind of argument going on, and Jay was desperately trying to win it.

Lissa got up and carried the baby to the kitchen, sidling close to the door and straining her ears. She made a pretense of clearing off the kitchen table one-handedly, but her movement stilled every time she heard the voices again. She couldn't make out what Jay was saying, but his tone conveyed wheedling.

Finally the argument was resolved—at least she supposed it was—and someone knocked on her door. *Now what?*

Jay stood by himself when she opened it.

"Is it time for your cookie break?" she asked, smiling.

"Nope," he assured her. "I want to be plenty hungry for pizza. Dad says to invite you." He wrinkled his forehead and reconsidered. "No, he said *I* should invite you and not mention him."

"Oh. Well. In that case, I'd be delighted to join you for pizza."

Jay broke into a grin. "Great! Come on and see what the place looks like."

Lissa balanced the baby in one arm, nudged her door shut and followed him across the hall. The door to the other apartment was ajar, and Lissa could hear Joe moving around inside.

Lissa was behind Jay when he stopped in the kitchen. Joe looked up and Lissa watched his expression alter. He met her eyes and then his own slid away. He was wearing a baseball cap, slightly askew, and Lissa couldn't stop her eyes from traveling over his old red sweatshirt with the cutoff arms and his faded jeans. The man could sure do a lot for jeans.

"I was invited for dinner," she said hesitantly, beginning to wonder if she'd made a mistake in accepting Jay's invitation.

"Dinner. Yeah." Joe looked at her again, but she couldn't read his expression. She wasn't at all sure what her own face revealed. She was unsure around him, and she was wary of the powerful emotions he seemed able to summon from her at will. Anger, passion, regret.

Defensive. She was definitely defensive, Joe thought, watching her eyes skitter around the room and light on everything but him. He was sure she fully expected to put up with more of his censure, but she was here anyway. She had guts. The lady hadn't flinched from a fight since he'd met her.

"We're ordering pizza, Dad," Jay piped up.

"We are?" Joe teased him, pretending to forget. "But I have all the ingredients for this wonderful veal roulade."

"Veal!" Jay looked panicked. "But, Dad, you said pizza." Joe's mouth twitched, and Jay realized he'd been getting the business. "Great, Dad," he said dryly. "Give your only son a heart attack."

"So what do you think of the place?" Joe said, turning his attention back to Lissa.

Lissa slowly looked around at the broken tile, chipped and fading paint, cracked windows, dangling curtain rods, killer dust bunnies and in the midst of all that Joe and Jay's pile of belongings.

"I think if we hurry, we could get a United Nations relief force in here," she murmured.

"Can't you see the potential?" Joe said incredulously. "Look at those window seats, that woodwork."

She looked, and she saw cracked, peeling wood and a spiderweb farm, but it made her smile to know that Joe saw potential.

"I think your potential is a little rotted," she told him.

"I can fix that," he informed her, and she wanted to smile again in the face of his assurance. He was supremely self-confident, whether he was dealing with building a bridge, fixing up an apartment or loving his son. Or dealing with a woman. Abruptly, Lissa turned her attention from that train of thought and focused instead on the paper bags sitting on the floor.

"Do you really need that much food?" she asked.

"It's all weird stuff," Jay informed her. "Dad's got more spices than I've got bugs in my bug collection."

"My son the food critic," Joe groused, but the corners of his mouth twitched. "And keep your bug collection out of my kitchen." His eyes rested on Lissa again. "What I need now is someone to put it away while I set up the bedrooms. It wouldn't take that long, and I'd owe you a good dinner."

Lissa looked at one of the open cupboards and then back to Joe. "This kitchen should be condemned. I'm not putting good food in those cupboards just so the spiders can carry it off."

Joe raised one eyebrow. "You're saying the cupboards need work?"

"They sure do. They could use a good cleaning and then maybe a coat of paint and shelf paper." She was ticking the items off on her fingers when she looked at Joe and saw him grinning at her.

"Shelf paper?" he asked innocently.

"All right," she sighed. "I've got some leftover shelf paper in my apartment. I'll take care of your cupboards."

"I'll owe you two dinners," he promised her.

Jay watched the baby while Lissa tackled the cupboards. They were a certifiable disaster area, and she scrunched up her face as she wiped out the inside with a sponge and her rubber glove-covered hand. "Look at that!" she said accusingly to Joe the next time he wandered past. She had taken off the glove and now dangled it from her fingertips. It was blackened and covered with smudges and cobwebs. "I want hazardous-duty pay for this."

"A pizza with everything on it that your heart desires," he promised her, his eyes lingering on her as he passed. She was kneeling on the floor, and her jeans were tight around her thighs. She could feel his gaze, as warm as if he'd touched her. She turned back to the cupboard, glancing up once to find him in the bedroom doorway, frowning as he watched her. When she met his eyes, he lowered his head and moved on, carrying the cot into the bedroom.

She wondered what he was thinking. She'd expected her own anger at him to last. But it had evaporated as soon as he'd looked at her tonight, leaving her empty and longing for something she told herself she couldn't have.

"Time to order the pizzas!" Joe announced two hours later, and Lissa stood, dusting off her jeans and standing back a moment to admire the yellow gingham shelf paper she'd installed.

"I want the works!" Jay announced from a sitting position on the living-room floor where he held Suzanne on his lap and simultaneously watched TV. "Except no yucky green peppers or stinky little fish!"

Joe held up his hands. "Two large pizzas," he said. "And Lissa gets to pick the toppings."

She could feel Jay's hopeful eyes on her as she turned. "All right," she said, discomfited enough by Joe's gaze to continue brushing her hands against her jeans. "I've decided. The works—but no green peppers and no anchovies."

"Yes!" Jay cried, leaping to a standing position with the baby in one arm while he pulled in the elbow of his other arm and pumped. "Yes!" Suzanne, ever the flirt, burbled and cooed as he jiggled her up and down.

"I've got the water faucet fixed in the bathroom sink," Joe said, "if anyone needs to wash up." He gave Jay a significant glance, and Jay sighed elaborately.

"Sure, Dad. You mean me, right?" Sighing again, he handed the baby to Joe and trotted off.

"I'll call in the pizza order," Lissa volunteered, avoiding Joe's eyes as she hurried to her own apartment.

When she got back, Jay had found his video game in a box, and Joe had hooked up a small TV and a VCR in the living room for him to play. Lissa settled on the floor near Joe, watching Jay systematically demolish some kind of dragon that kept reappearing.

"You packed a VCR?" Lissa said to Joe.

He shrugged. "Jay needs some entertainment. I take him in the summers as much as I can, even when I go out of town on jobs. I don't want him to get bored."

Lissa couldn't imagine anyone being bored around Joe, but she supposed that was the kind of thing a father worried about.

"What does he do while you're at work?" she asked curiously.

"He usually stays with someone," Joe said. "Jay's already met a kid his age down the street. There's a grandmother home all day, and I'm going to pay her to look after Jay on the days he doesn't want to hang around the site with me."

She thought it must be hard on him trying to live a normal home life with his son when he was on an out-of-town job, but then, what did she know about a normal home life?

The pizza arrived, interrupting her thoughts. The two males were ravenous, but they still insisted that Lissa eat the last piece, despite her claims that she was about to burst. "Go ahead and burst," Joe advised her as he handed her the final slice. "I plan to repaint the walls anyway."

She gave him a you-asked-for-it look and took a bite as Joe and Jay dived for cover, their arms shielding their heads.

"Good one, Dad," Jay laughed as he rolled over onto his back.

Joe rumpled Jay's hair and gave him a light punch on the arm. "All right, son. It's time you started getting cleaned up."

"Already?" Jay complained. "It's only—" he grabbed Joe's arm and checked his watch "—five-fifteen."

"Somewhere in the world, but not in this apartment," Joe assured him. He looked at Lissa and shrugged. "I was afraid Mrs. McGee would wonder why I wasn't wearing the watch she fixed."

"Hey, Dad, I don't need to get cleaned up," Jay said as inspiration struck him. "I don't have any clean clothes anyway, remember?"

"Aw, geez!" Joe said. "I meant to do that laundry tonight." He ran a hand through his hair. "Listen," he said to Lissa, "you said there's a washer in the basement, didn't you?"

"A dryer, too," she told him. "I'll show you how to work it if you'd like. It can be a little temperamental."

"Yeah, great. Thanks." Joe gathered up a load of clothes, stuffed them into a duffel bag and sent Jay to the bathroom to begin washing for bed. "And don't forget to brush your teeth," he called over his shoulder as he followed Lissa out the door.

Lissa pulled the string attached to the one hanging bulb in the basement and stood just outside the pool of light jiggling the baby as she watched Joe take clothes from the duffel bag and dump them into the washer.

"You're going to wash all those things in the same load?" she asked skeptically as she saw a pair of dark blue jeans fall on top of some of Jay's white undershorts.

He flashed her a rueful smile over his shoulder. "One thing I've learned as a single father is compromise," he informed her. "Jay and I've come to love pastel-colored underwear."

Lissa watched him set the temperature controls and turn the knob on the washer. "You have to twist it twice," she told him. "It's kind of like a safe. You need the right combination. There, that's it. Now thump it on top."

He looked skeptical, but he followed her directions. The washer started.

Joe leaned back against it and studied Lissa.

"The diaper service came by yesterday," she said hesitantly. "Thank you."

Joe nodded. "Why haven't you been using my car?" he demanded when she didn't say anything else.

She didn't want to get into an argument with him over it, but she didn't want him thinking he could run her life, either. Taking a deep breath, she said, "I like my car. It's seen me through a lot of crises, and I figure the least I can do is return the favor."

"For God's sake, Lissa!" he exploded, pushing himself away from the washer and stalking toward her. She shrank back even farther from the pool of light, and he halted, a dark frown on his face. The bare bulb cast angular shadows on his face. "It's a hunk of tin! You feel loyalty for a car, and you didn't have any for a man?"

"That's right!" she snapped back, goaded beyond endurance by his words. "I'm cold and heartless and selfish, and I don't give a damn about anyone else! Satisfied? Isn't that what you want to hear, Joe?"

"No," he said sharply, taking another step toward her. His head struck the hanging bulb, sending it careening wildly back and forth. The shadows advanced and retreated on his face, like clouds rolling over the sun. The anger seemed to seep out of him as he stared back at her, and he closed his eyes briefly. "No," he said again, quietly. "That's not what I want to hear."

"Then what?" she demanded, her own voice soft and unsure.

Joe shrugged impatiently. He couldn't answer her. He didn't know himself what he wanted from her. He was consumed with need whenever he looked at her, the need to hold her and touch her and bury himself deeply inside her. And that need made him lash out at her. He was feeling things for Lissa that made a mockery of his carefully controlled emotions. He'd learned a lesson in self-preservation at the hands of his ex-wife, and he'd built himself a tidy world with tidy emotions since then. Jay was the only person he'd invested his feelings in. He hadn't had so much as an inkling of his own vulnerability until he'd met this woman.

He shrugged again. "Hell, I don't know." But he did. He wanted to hear her say that she wanted him as badly as he wanted her.

She stared at him a moment longer, assessing, trying to understand, and then Suzanne whimpered. Lissa settled the baby against her shoulder. "I have to go. It's getting late, and Suzanne should be in bed."

"I'll come with you," he said when she turned to go.

He hadn't been able to think of much else but her the past two days, and consequently he hadn't had much sleep. He was tired and dirty, but still he knew he didn't want to tell her good-night just yet.

"What's this?" he asked as they crossed the floor toward the door. He'd already turned out the hanging light, but like lace the dim glow from the streetlight outside lay on an old rocking chair sticking up from a pile of odds and ends near the door.

Lissa stopped and waited. "It's Mrs. McGee's. One of the rockers is broken. She was going to throw it away, but it ended up here in her junk pile."

"I could fix it," Joe said, hauling the rocker out of the pile and bending close to inspect it. "Do you think she'd mind?"

"No, of course not," Lissa said. "It would be nice in your apartment."

"I was thinking more of yours," he said, ignoring her look of surprise as he hefted the chair and started for the stairs to the apartments.

Lissa followed him, at a loss. He kept her constantly off balance. He made everything he told her sound like an order, and then he'd turn around and do something nice. Although some of the nice things he did sounded like orders, too, she remembered irritably.

"I need to give Suzanne a quick bath," Lissa said inside her apartment. Joe had left the rocker on the landing and followed her.

"I'll help," he offered, wanting to be with her and wondering if she would put up much of an objection. But she merely shrugged, and he recognized the protective shell she was throwing up around herself. She was holding the baby against her shoulder, and Suzanne had grabbed a fistful of her mother's blouse, pulling it away from her neck. Joe thought Lissa's bare throat and collarbone looked awfully tempting, especially with that little knit top she was wearing. He forced himself to look away.

He followed her to the sink and watched while she put down a rubber mat, then ran the water. She passed the baby to him, and he smiled as Suzanne clutched his shirt and babbled softly, lowering her mouth to the fabric. As if it were yesterday, he could remember holding Jay like this. He loved babies, but he might as well forget about any more, because there was no way he was going to let any woman do to him what his ex-wife had done.

Then he glanced up and met Lissa's eyes, and it hit him in the stomach like a load of concrete that if she kept looking at him like that, all soft and vulnerable, he was never going to keep in mind what marriage had done to him.

She tested the water with her elbow, then took Suzanne from him and laid her in her infant carrier to undress her. Apparently, a bath was one of the baby's favorite activities, because she cooed and laughed as Lissa lowered her into the water.

Suzanne began to splash, and Lissa smiled. "Now, isn't that fun?" she said, picking up the washcloth. "Joe, would you hand me the soap?"

He reached for the soap, realizing that he was feeling things he hadn't felt for years. He was standing close to a woman and her baby, participating in that normal event called bathtime, and he was suddenly realizing how much he'd missed it.

"Why don't you soap her?" Lissa suggested.

Joe hesitated, then stepped forward and began lathering Suzanne. She loved it, and Lissa laughed softly. He glanced at her and immediately forgot what he was doing. She looked so warm and sexy standing there.

The laughter died on her lips, and she stared back at him. "I'll do it," she said softly, taking the soap from him. Her fingers grazed his and immediately slipped away. Lowering her eyes, she bathed Suzanne, not looking at him again.

He was standing close, and she could feel her pulse take off as though she were some crazy kid in love and totally devoid of sense. She could feel his reaction, as well, and it surprised her to realize that he was dealing with his own case of nerves.

He was holding the towel when she'd rinsed off the baby, and Lissa passed the kicking and grinning child to his arms. "Now, wasn't that great?" she murmured with a smile to her delighted daughter.

Her eyes briefly met his, and they both looked away. Lissa badly wanted to ask him to leave or ask him to stay, she didn't know which, but whatever feelings were warring inside her, she thought she might scream if he didn't say something to her soon. She was aching for his touch; just looking at him made her knees go weak. She needed his sarcasm to keep her longing at bay.

He dried off Suzanne, who gurgled and cooed, and he followed Lissa to the crib in the alcove. The baby was wearing down now that her bath was over, and she smiled sleepily after Lissa put on a fresh diaper and her sleeper and laid her in the crib. Lissa touched a finger to her cheek and brushed back a tiny strand of hair. "Sleep tight, little one," she whispered.

Suzanne's eyes drifted nearly closed, but she managed a soft, "Boo," that ended on a sigh.

Lissa turned and met Joe's eyes, and suddenly she was scared. She couldn't make sense of the simmering feeling of anticipation that leaped from one nerve ending to another like bursts of lightning. She didn't know what she was getting into, but she couldn't turn away from it, either. Releasing her breath, she looked away from the enigmatic brown eyes studying her face.

Silently Joe followed her to the kitchen. The ceiling fixture was low-wattage and gave off only a soft glow, casting a pool of gauzy luminescence onto the table like a lace doily. They both stood awkwardly.

She looked so pretty despite the almost desperate wariness in her eyes. She still didn't trust him, and he acknowledged that he'd given her no reason to do so. He'd pretty much given her nothing but hell since he'd set eyes on her.

He supposed she still wanted him out of her life, but that was no longer an option for him.

In the silence, he could hear the loud, frenetic ticking of that damn cat clock. It was just like the woman, he thought, to offer up every timepiece she owned for Mrs. McGee's destructive instincts.

"Would you like some coffee or something?" she offered finally, badly wanting to know what he was thinking.

Or something. That pretty much summed it up, he decided. He wanted something from Lissa Gray, and he suspected that he wanted more than she was willing to give him.

"No," he said when he wanted to say yes. "I have to be down at the site early tomorrow. I really should go, besides, I need to check on Jay. I'll get that rocker fixed for you."

He was exhausted. She could see it in the lines at his eyes and the set of his shoulders. He'd worked on his job all day and then on the apartment all night. She suspected that he kept moving, kept himself occupied so he wouldn't have to think too much about something. But what? What was it that drove Joe Douglas?

"Well, I need a cup of tea," she said, turning away from him, needing to keep her hands busy. She put a mug of water into the microwave. "I like to go out on the balcony at night with my tea and sit. I got into the habit when I was pregnant with Suzanne and I needed to think about…" Her words trailed off awkwardly. When she needed to think about what was going to happen to her life. "The rocker will be nice," she said quietly.

"Lissa," he said from behind her, his voice low and urgent. She turned around and found herself only inches from him. His dark eyes bore the same intensity she'd heard in his voice. "I don't want this," he said, even as his hands closed on her shoulders and pulled her close to him.

"I don't either," she managed to breathe before his mouth came down on hers and swallowed her last word.

She'd been waiting so long for this, so long for him to touch her and kiss her with this kind of need. She couldn't get enough of him. Her arms wrapped themselves around his neck, and she arched against him.

He raised his mouth long enough to take a quick, shaky breath, and then he was kissing her again with all the hunger of a man who couldn't help himself. His roughened hands sought her waist and slid beneath the pink shell, but they were gentle despite his urgency. When they cupped her breasts, she pressed into him, her nipples hardening as his thumbs stroked them.

"Lissa," he groaned, but his hands communicated what he didn't say. He wanted her. He wanted her so much that he would put aside all his principles and all his doubts just to touch her like this.

She kissed his hard jaw and his face, moaning when he lowered his head to bury his mouth against her throat. The beginnings of his beard scratched her neck, but it only inflamed her desire, and her breath came in soft, sharp exhalations against his hair. He smelled so good, she thought, the scent of hard work and maleness, realizing she hadn't been this close to a man in such a long time. Desperately, she communicated her need as Joe ran his hands down her back and cupped her bottom.

He raised his head and looked at her quizzically, his forehead furrowed. She didn't even know she was crying until he raised a hand and grazed her cheek with his thumb. He stood stock-still, though his breathing was harsh. "Lissa?" he said quietly. His other hand rested on her arm, and he didn't move it.

"I don't...know what's wrong," she said helplessly. And she didn't.

"I'd better go," he said, his thumb gently stroking away her tears. "It's getting late." He seemed loath to let go of her, though, and quickly he pulled her against him and rested his head on her hair. They stood that way a long minute, and then he finally put her away from him.

He walked to the door, and she couldn't take her eyes from him. He was such a good-looking man, and he had the kind of strength that nothing could shake. She could use some of that strength tonight for herself.

"Joe." She hadn't meant to say his name with such aching need. When he turned, she didn't know what to tell him. *Stay with me.* They had both wanted the same thing a minute ago, and now the moment was irretrievably gone.

"It's all right," he told her with a wry smile that didn't reach his eyes. She could see the tightness in his jaw. "Things aren't…easy between us, are they, Lissa? It's a hell of a situation we're in. I don't know why things happen the way they do sometimes." His eyes locked with hers, and she could feel his tension. She wanted to hold him, but something in his face kept her standing where she was. "I used to have a little girl, too," he said, the words hard, as though his throat hurt as they forced their way past. "I used to sit in a rocker with her when she cried at night." He looked like he couldn't say any more, and then he did. "Maybe that's why things are so hard between us. I keep fighting the past."

He left then, and she stared at the door. Dear God. What private hell had he gone through?

Six

———

The rain woke Lissa toward morning, and she got up to close the window, first standing there a moment to inhale the fresh, wet scent. She couldn't sleep after that, so she pulled on her robe and went to the kitchen.

She filled a mug with water and opened the microwave, sighing when she saw the mug of water left from last night. She could still see him, the way he'd looked at her before he left. If he'd come back to her at that moment, she would have taken him to her bed, despite the bitterness between them.

She couldn't do this, she thought for the hundredth time. She couldn't bear having Joe right next door, so close she could open her door and call to him in the middle of the night—if she wanted.

This was too hard.

And the difficulties were compounded by what he'd said last night. He'd had a little girl of his own. Lissa had lain awake a good part of the night, staring at the ceiling and wondering what had happened. Was his loss the reason he was so intent on being a part of Suzanne's life? It could also be the reason he threatened to take custody of her baby. Lissa hugged her arms to herself and shivered. The Joe she was beginning to know wouldn't do that—would he?

Lissa had started a pot of coffee and was dressed in jeans and a turquoise blouse when someone knocked on the door at seven.

She knew it was Joe before she opened the door, some innate female sense thrumming with his nearness before she even set eyes on him.

"I seem to have run out of milk," he said with an apologetic shrug. "I was wondering if I could borrow some."

But it wasn't milk on either of their minds when he stepped inside. His eyes were glittering as they traveled over her, russet embers that burned every inch of her skin. She read his indecision and his pain.

"About last night..." he began hesitantly.

Lissa carefully kept her hands at her sides, despite the temptation to touch him, to urge him to draw her into his arms. When he frowned down at the floor and didn't go on, she gestured toward the table. "It's all right," she said. "I understand. You don't have to talk about it."

"But I do," he insisted, those fiery eyes swinging back to her face. He forced himself to sit down, then got to his feet almost immediately and began pacing the small kitchen.

Lissa could see his torment, and she knew that talking to her about it was costing him a great deal. She turned to the sink and absently fiddled with the dirty dishes, not wanting to bear witness to his suffering, but unable to do otherwise.

"It was the rocker," he said, pausing momentarily to touch a shiny magnet on the refrigerator. Lissa knew that in his mind's eye he was seeing something else, that like her he needed to keep his hands busy. "I used to get up with

Shanna—my little girl—at night and rock her. She had colic
and then she was teething. I spent a lot of time with her at
night, trying to soothe her and help her sleep."

He sighed, a wrenching sound that made Lissa's heart
clench. She knew what it was like to spend those midnight
hours with a baby. There was a special closeness then. "It
was Shanna who broke up our marriage," he said, resum-
ing his pacing again. "Caroline—my wife—didn't want
her."

"Even after she held her baby?" Lissa asked, unable to
keep from asking.

Joe nodded. "The first pregnancy with Jay had been hard
on her. The second was worse. She had to spend the last
three months in bed, and Caroline was the kind of woman
who couldn't stand that." He gave a brief, bitter smile. "She
was full of laughter when I met her, the life of the party. It
was what drew me to her. I didn't realize until after we were
married that she *was* the party. Caroline lived for excitement and fun. I didn't exactly give her those things, working away from home half the time and too tired to go out
socializing when I was there."

"Surely she didn't expect the same life after the children," Lissa protested. No sane woman could. Children
changed things irrevocably. Any fool knew that.

Joe didn't answer, and slowly Lissa dried her hands on the
dish towel and turned to face him. He was staring at the
wall, the pain on his face as blatant as a scarred brand. She
had to stifle the cry in her throat.

"If I wasn't home, she'd take the children with her when
she went out partying...." Joe said. His voice trailed off into
bitterness again. "She'd pack them into the car and leave
them there while she had a good time."

"My God," Lissa whispered in horror.

"One night I came home early from an out-of-town job
and she was gone. I looked all over the city for her." He

pressed his thumb against his forehead and massaged it as
though he could rub away the memory like a smudge. "I finally found the car parked outside a lounge across town.
Both kids were locked inside." His face hardened, and Lissa's breath caught in her throat. "It was five degrees out that
night. Jay already had a cold, and it went into bronchitis
after that." He took a deep shuddering breath and turned
his eyes on Lissa. They were hard and unforgiving. Like
dark, volcanic glass, his gaze pinned Lissa to the spot. "I
went inside that bar and dragged Caroline out by the hair,"
he said in a low, controlled voice that belied the heated anger smoldering beneath the surface. "I could have killed her
that night. We divorced as soon as I could push the paperwork through."

Something told Lissa that this wasn't the end of his story.
She hardly breathed as his features grew even more taut, his
mouth a thin, hard line. He had idly picked up a pencil she'd
left lying on the counter after making out her grocery list,
and now he worried it in his hand, turning it over and over
as though it held the secret to some great mystery.

Joe's voice sounded old and tired when he spoke again.
"Two weeks after the divorce, she went out again and left
Shanna in the car. The court had granted Caroline temporary custody until a permanent decision was reached. She
was a toddler—active, into everything. From what the po-
lice put together, my little girl bumped the gearshift into
neutral while she was playing alone. The car rolled down the
street and through a red light. Another car at the intersec-
tion plowed into it. Shanna's head hit the dashboard." Another shuddering breath escaped Joe and left Lissa aching
with shared misery. When those bottomless brown eyes
sought hers, something had gone out of them, leaving a
black void in its place. "She died two hours later at the
hospital. Jay was still quite young then, but I know he

misses Shanna just as much as I do. You can see how fraternal he is around Suzanne."

A loud crack broke the silence that followed his last sentence, and they both looked down at his hand where the pencil lay broken in two. His hand was shaking as he dropped the pieces onto the counter.

Lissa's knees felt weak, and she realized her hands were trembling. She'd listened to the story without interruption, because she knew he had to get it out, and even if that didn't exorcise his demons, it lessened the pain by some small degree. She'd wager he hadn't unburdened himself in a long time, maybe never. Joe wasn't the kind of man who went around crying on other people's shoulders.

She should know. She wasn't that kind of woman, either.

But maybe that was a point in her favor, because she understood what he was going through. And she could offer what little solace she had.

Quietly, slowly, she went to him. His eyes hadn't left her face, and he let her look into them now and see the anger and the grief and the broken heart. She took his measure, and then she reached out gently and cupped his jaw in her hand.

Joe shuddered once, as though throwing off the last of the horror, and then his body uncoiled like wire when the tension is released. His arms came around Lissa, pulling her to him, and she heard a choked sound deep in his chest.

She did the only thing she could, held him and murmured softly, words of comfort. He rocked her in his arms, his dark head bent to hers, his breathing harsh and warm against her hair.

"I haven't told anyone about that in a long time," he murmured hoarsely.

"I know," she whispered. "I know."

"It still hurts," he ground out after a short silence. Gently he held her away from him and studied her face. "Lissa, I don't give trust easily and I don't ask it of anyone."

Her fingers clung to his arms, hungry for the feel of him. "You had little reason to expect your trust to be respected," she said, trying to sound rational when all she wanted to do was fling herself into his arms again. "What happened to you would kill most people."

"You don't understand," he said, his hands holding her steady, his eyes never leaving her face. "I changed after what happened. I'm not such a good risk for anyone now. I play by my own rules and I make sure I don't get hurt."

He was right—she didn't understand. "What do you mean?"

"I mean that if I were you, I'd stay as far away from me as you can get. Sweetheart, you're probably thinking to yourself now that I'm just some gruff guy, misunderstood but with a heart of gold. Well, I'm not. I don't let myself be taken in by anything or anyone, and I'm a hell of a lot rougher on relationships than any man you've met in your lifetime. I've paid my dues, and I'm through paying."

"So what else is new?" she demanded, finding the resilience to show him her own strength.

Her reward was a wry smile. "Yeah, well remember that. I've given you warning."

He started to release her, then seemed to change his mind. She leaned toward him, but someone chose that moment to knock on the door.

Joe swore. "Probably Jay."

But it was Bonnie Ann, looking confused and guilty when she looked past Lissa and saw Joe. "I was just..." she began, flushing.

"I've got to get going," Joe said, checking his watch and scowling when he remembered it was now little more than a man's bracelet, certainly not a timepiece.

He brushed past Lissa, giving her one last look that spoke volumes, and nodded to Bonnie Ann. Neither Joe nor Lissa remembered the milk he'd wanted to borrow.

"Whew!" Bonnie Ann said when the door had closed behind him. "Was there a fire in here or is all that heat just my imagination?"

"I was getting the Joe Douglas Rules of Life," Lissa said, trying to sound lighthearted and not succeeding. She understood that Joe was trying to protect her in some way by warning her away from him, but he was wrong. She'd gotten a glimpse of the man underneath that rough exterior and she was more intrigued than ever. "What are you doing out at this hour?" she asked Bonnie Ann, changing the subject.

"Just happened to be in the neighborhood and thought I'd drop off some class notes I typed up," Bonnie Ann said. "I got up early this morning so I could make cinnamon rolls for breakfast. Then I decided to go for a jog. Did I tell you I'm starting a new exercise program? I jog three miles a day." Bonnie Ann glanced longingly at the coffeepot. "Could I have a cup? I'll wring out the grounds if it's all gone."

"No need," Lissa assured her. She poured them each a cup and leaned against the counter sipping.

Bonnie Ann took a large swallow and closed her eyes in satisfaction. "Good and strong," she said approvingly, opening her eyes to study Lissa and beginning to pace the kitchen in her usual hyperactive style. "So, what's happening with Joe?"

"What do you mean?" Lissa asked, pretending ignorance.

"I mean, what's going on between you two?"

Lissa became suddenly interested in her coffee cup. "I don't know."

"All right," Bonnie Ann said. "It's none of my business." It was obvious to Lissa that she didn't really believe that. "Listen," she said, "I just don't want you to get hurt."

"I know," Lissa said. "And I appreciate it. Believe me." She could still sense her friend's discomfort, and she frowned. "What is it, Bonnie Ann?"

Bonnie Ann sighed. "I talked to my cousin. Sherry? Remember?"

The one who knew all the gossip. Lissa could feel her throat tightening. "And?"

"Did you know Joe had a daughter?"

Lissa nodded. "She was killed in an accident. He told me what happened."

Bonnie Ann looked skeptical. "All of it?"

"What do you mean?" Suddenly the room seemed ten degrees cooler.

"After his little girl was killed, Joe sought custody of his son. Did he tell you that?"

Lissa shook her head. She'd assumed when Joe told her his story that Jay was already living with Joe. "That seems like a reasonable thing to do after what happened," she said.

"He hired a lawyer, a man named Cassidy. He's a big gun around these parts. One of those hotshots who specializes in divorces and custody. They say his clients are never disappointed in his results. From what Sherry said, this Cassidy dragged Joe's ex-wife through the mud or threatened to. It never made it as a full court case. Apparently, just Cassidy's and Joe's threats were enough to make the ex-wife sign over full custody to Joe." Bonnie Ann took another deep swallow of her coffee. "He played hardball, Lissa. And from what Sherry said, he didn't flinch. I just thought you ought to know... and be careful."

Lissa nodded. "Okay. Thanks, Bonnie Ann."

Bonnie Ann drained the last of her coffee and trotted to the door. "You take care, honey. I've got to go finish my jog. It helps me sleep at night."

Lissa didn't personally believe anything but a strong whack on the head could make Bonnie Ann sleep at night, but she gave her a weak smile and shut the door.

Joe had warned her of as much, but she hadn't believed him. Wearily, she rubbed her temple in an unconscious imitation of Joe's gesture. The trouble was, she already felt that she was in too deep.

Worn and edgy, Lissa trooped up the stairs that evening, convinced that the day had taken on the personality of a mugger, and it had smacked her around in pretty good fashion. Suzanne was nestled in one arm, fussing and squirming, and it was all Lissa could do to balance her with the books and sack of groceries in her other arm. Lissa's hair was damp and curling from the rain, and a lock over her eyes kept dripping onto her nose.

A shaft of gray light intersected the stairs as the door above opened, and Joe called, "Hey, you need some help?"

"No," she said dryly. "I'm learning juggling in one easy lesson."

He was at her side in two seconds flat, taking the things from her arms, leaving her to soothe the baby while he took her key and unlocked the door.

He looked good, she thought, feeling her mouth grow dry in response. His jeans hugged his hips and thighs, and that black, shortsleeved shirt emphasized his hard chest and arms.

Once they were inside she waited for him to say something—*anything*—that would help her gauge his mood. She had no idea how he would feel about her after his confession that morning.

He put down the groceries and books, then took the baby and held the child against his shoulder, walking back and forth and murmuring until Suzanne quieted.

Lissa dropped onto a kitchen chair and studied him. "How was *your* day?" she finally asked quietly as he set Suzanne in her infant carrier and tickled her chin with a forefinger.

"Not bad," he said mildly. "It rained like the devil, so I couldn't get anything done but paperwork, and even that was hopeless since no one had gotten the cement figures I needed. Oh, yeah. And some lunkhead ran into me with a piece of steel."

"Were you hurt badly?" Lissa shifted in her seat as he shook his head and met her eyes. He was letting her look into them again, letting her see what he was feeling. She could read the need, and it made her feel lightheaded. She was amazed at her own weakness for him. A word, a look, and she tumbled.

Discussing her day seemed safer ground than staring into Joe's eyes. "I had a lousy day," she sighed. "Some jerk got too close to the curb and sprayed me with mud. And then I got in the car, and my panty hose tore. The milkshake maker broke at Duncans'—in the middle of a milkshake—and there was a pop quiz in history—on a chapter I hadn't read—and I got a C-minus."

There was a brief silence. "A C-minus?" he repeated, his brows going up. "You didn't read the chapter and you got a C-minus? I'm impressed."

He lowered himself into the chair opposite her, and she frowned, noting that he looked tired and hassled himself.

"It's not that impressive," she assured him.

"Then I guess I have to come up with another excuse to take you out for dinner," he said, stretching tentatively as if he was stiff and achy.

He watched her sitting there so composed and still that nothing betrayed what she was thinking. Finally, she dropped her eyes from his and traced her finger over a smudge on the table. The light caught her gold hoop earrings, and he felt his mouth go dry with desire. He knew that he'd just warned her away from him this morning, but he couldn't seem to help himself where she was concerned. He wanted to be with her.

She glanced at the window. "I don't know. It's still raining."

"Tell you what then. I'll fix us something here."

"You're tired," she protested.

"I can manage," he assured her. "And I'll get Jay to help. Besides, I promised you a *couple* of dinners." He suspected that part of her reluctance might stem from her fear of their being alone together. He decided he was right when he saw her visibly relax.

"All right," she said, giving in. "I was going to make beef stew tonight, but your offer sounds better." What he did for a pair of jeans was criminal, she thought again, and he didn't seem to have any idea what effect he had on her. "Don't go to much trouble," she told him. "Just something simple."

"Yeah, right."

It may have been a simple dinner for Joe, but to Lissa it was a gourmet feast. He used her stew meat to produce a superlative beef Burgundy, and while that was cooking, he and Jay put together a salad of lettuce, artichoke hearts, mushrooms, garlic and olive oil. From his apartment he produced some crusty rolls, and apples and pears for dessert.

"This defies mere words," Lissa assured him when she sat down at the table. Joe settled Suzanne in her high-chair and positioned it next to Lissa.

Smiling, he poured her a glass of red wine. Jay settled for apple juice.

"You aren't having any?" she asked as he put the bottle aside.

"My tastes run more to beer," he said.

"Now that I can supply," Lissa said, getting a cold bottle from the refrigerator. She held up her offering so Joe could read the label and he murmured his approval.

"I know you said you could cook, but *this* . . ." she said appreciatively as she dug into the food. "This is unbelievable. I'm more than impressed. I don't mean to gush, but I haven't had a meal like this since, well, longer than I can remember."

"Oh, go ahead and gush," he encouraged her, and Lissa laughed.

Jay wasn't overly enthusiastic about the meal, but he perked up when Lissa offered him a supplementary peanut butter sandwich to go with his milk.

Joe and Jay set about doing the dishes after dinner while Lissa got the baby ready for bed. From the alcove bedroom she watched Jay grin and elbow Joe. "What?" Joe groused.

"I never saw you in an apron before, Dad," Jay said, his grin widening as he looked at his father.

"It's not an apron, son," Joe insisted. "It's a large tea towel, and Lissa made me wear it so I wouldn't get Burgundy sauce on my jeans."

"Yeah, sure, Dad. It's not an apron. It just looks like one." Jay put another dish in the cupboard and leaned over to switch on the radio on the counter, fiddling with the tuning knob until rock music blasted forth.

Joe carefully dried his hands on the towel around his waist, crossed his arms and leaned a hip against the sink. "Now, Son, don't give me a hard time about the ap—towel or I'll be forced to withhold your allowance until you're close to retirement and need it for your IRA. And change the radio station. That is not appropriate dishwashing music."

"Yessir," Jay said, but his smile was still firmly in place.

"Now that's more like it," Joe said when Jay found a blues station, one that Lissa liked to listen to herself on rainy nights when the baby was asleep.

Lissa laid Suzanne in the crib, turning on the musical mobile when she fussed. Suzanne focused on the slowly turning mobile and quieted, her lids drooping over her eyes. A minute later she was asleep, and Lissa tiptoed from the room, gently closing the door.

"There you are," Joe said. "The dishes are done. Want another glass of wine?"

"Maybe a small one," she allowed, basking in a feeling of contentment.

Joe kept looking at her, but he tried to be inconspicuous about it. He liked that turquoise blouse. Hell, he liked everything about her. The way the light sifted through her hair, turning it to spun gold, the way her blue eyes deepened when she was happy or sad, the cute little wiggle she had when she walked. And the patient, comforting way she'd listened to him this morning. The tender way her arms had gone around him, it might have been her own heart that was broken.

He'd like to do more than cook a dinner for her. He'd like to take her to his bed and make love to her until those blue eyes widened in heartrending pleasure. He'd like to put a blissful smile on her face from the most thorough lovemaking she'd ever experienced.

But he had to remember; his marriage had made him a hard man, a man who knew how to look after himself. He was right to have warned her away from him. He wasn't always the kindest of men, as she well knew. And he was single-minded when it came to doing what he had to do.

"Hey, Dad," Jay said, drawing him back from his reverie. "Did I tell you my friend Stuart's having a birthday party next month?"

"No kidding," Joe said. "Isn't Stuart the one who takes tap dancing lessons?"

"Yeah," Jay said with thinly disguised disgust. "He says his mom's going to play records and make us dance with the girls and weird stuff like that."

"You going?" Joe asked.

"I guess so," Jay said after thinking about it. "His dad owns a miniature golf course, so it might be worth having to dance and everything."

Joe laughed. "It's nice to know you can be bribed, son."

Jay shrugged, but grinned. "Dad?"

"What is it?"

"Do you know how to dance?"

"Yeah. Why? Do you think you might need lessons?"

"I guess so. There's this girl—Angie." Jay cast an embarrassed glance at Lissa, cleared his throat and continued. "I thought...you know...that if I *had* to dance anyway..."

"That you might as well be good enough at it to impress Angie," Joe finished for him. "That about right?"

"Just about," Jay confirmed.

"Tell you what. Why don't you ask Lissa to take a spin around the dance floor with you? That way you'll be an experienced man when the party rolls around."

Jay looked at Lissa hopefully. "Would you?" he asked. "I mean, if I promise not to stomp your feet or anything."

"I'd be honored," she said, smiling. She was tired, but she liked Jay, and dancing with him seemed very appealing after the rough day she'd had. She stood and held her arms out to the boy. She had to lean slightly to accommodate his smaller size, and he moved awkwardly into position.

Lissa readjusted his hands, then gave him an approving smile. "Very good. Now, start with your left foot and take one step forward." She continued coaching him through the box step as a velvety Harry Connick tune played on the radio. At first she guided Jay, but then, as he caught on, she let him lead.

"Look, Dad!" he crowed proudly. "I'm dancing!"

"So you are," Joe agreed affably.

"Here, you dance with her now," Jay said, pulling Lissa over to the table.

"I don't know, son," Joe said reluctantly. "It's been a long day. Lissa probably needs a little rest."

"But she's not old like Grandma," Jay protested. "She's not that tired, are you, Lissa?"

"Suddenly I feel totally revived," she admitted wryly. "Must be all that talk about age."

"There, see?" Jay told his dad. "Come on, Dad. Dance with her. Don't act old."

"How can I resist a gibe like that?" Joe said, shaking his head. He got to his feet and smiled at Lissa. "Care to dance with an old man?"

"I don't see any around," she said, pretending to search the kitchen. "But I think you'll do just fine."

Joe grinned at her and took her in his arms. They moved awkwardly at first, Lissa far too aware of Joe's touch, his warm hand at her back making her knees weak. The song on the radio ended, fading into a Dinah Washington song, slow and bluesy and ripe with longing.

"I like Dinah Washington," she said, desperate for any kind of conversation as she swayed with his body pressed so closely to hers. It was obvious to her that he was aroused, and he wasn't making any effort to hide it. That knowledge made her tremble.

"What else do you like?" he asked in a soft voice.

You. I'm afraid I like you far too much.

"Rainy nights," she said in a voice that sounded strained even to herself. "The smile on my baby's face when she sees me first thing in the morning."

"You're dancing too *slow*, Dad," Jay protested, looking up at them with a frown. "Heck, she's going to go to sleep on you."

"I hate critics," Joe murmured.

"C'mon, Dad, let me dance with her again." Jay pulled at his father's shirt and Joe winced.

"Take it easy on your old man's back, Jay."

"Oh, yeah, I forgot. Man, you should see the bruise he got!" Jay told Lissa. Joe was still holding her in his arms, but they'd stopped dancing. "It's about a foot long and twenty different colors!" Jay announced proudly.

"It's not as bad as all that," Joe said when Lissa looked at him worriedly. "Two of the guys were moving a beam and not paying attention to where they were going. I'm just a little stiff."

"It was bleeding and everything," Jay waxed on.

"Son, women don't like their dance partners to be such . . . enthusiastic conversationalists," Joe explained patiently.

"Huh?"

"Lissa doesn't want a full-blown description of my back, do you, Lissa?"

"No," she agreed. "I want to take a look at it in case you've done some real damage."

"What?"

"Don't look so outraged," she told him as she pulled him to the chair. "This will only take a minute."

"I'm *not* hurt," he insisted, letting her push him into the chair nevertheless.

"I'm sure of that," she agreed.

"Then why—"

"Because you shouldn't deny a woman a chance to see a bruise that's twenty different colors," she assured him.

She was giving him the business, and he found that he kind of liked it. Grinning, he began to pull off his shirt.

If she thought he was devastating with all his clothes on, she found he was even more so bare-chested. Lissa sucked in her breath and tried to concentrate on his back as he obligingly leaned forward for her.

"It's really neat, isn't it?" Jay said, leaning close to her to get a look.

"Very nice," Lissa said dryly. It must hurt like hell, she thought. It was, true to Jay's earlier description, several shades of blue, red and purple, and it was also swollen. The skin was scraped and angry-looking in the middle of the bruise.

"Hey, Dad, can I go watch TV?" Jay asked, apparently no longer interested in his father's injury.

Joe checked his watch and gave Lissa a significant look. "What time have you got?" he asked.

"Don't look at me," Lissa said. "Mrs. McGee's worked on every timepiece I own."

"Okay, I guess so," Joe told Jay. "Lock the door, and don't let anyone in except me."

Jay took off, and Joe sighed. "You wouldn't happen to have another beer around, would you?" he asked Lissa. "I think I'm going to need it."

"I've got one," she said. "And why do you think you need it?"

"Something tells me you're going to go messing with my back, aren't you?"

Without comment, Lissa got a beer from the refrigerator and handed it to him. "Turn around on the chair so I can reach your back," she told him.

"I *knew* you were going to mess with my back," he groused, twisting the cap from the bottle and taking a long swallow. He gave her a reproachful look, but he turned around so that he was straddling the back of the chair and leaned his forearms over it. His chest was firm and matted with dark hair, and she tried her best not to stare at it. Abruptly she went into the bathroom to get a washcloth.

She saw him wince when she touched the damp cloth to the bruise, and she cleaned it as gently as she could. She'd dislodged some crusted blood and now a few tiny fresh drops oozed from the scrape.

She blotted them and then looked at the Mercurochrome in her hand. "This might sting a little," she lied and quickly touched the applicator to the cut.

"Godalmighty!" he roared, sitting bolt upright in the chair. "What the hell is that?!"

"Mercurochrome," she said.

"Well, *blow* on it or something! Good Lord, Gray! I thought you'd knifed me."

"Sorry." She fanned his back with a napkin from the table, and he gradually relaxed. "Here, take these," she said, dropping two aspirin into his hand. She went to get a glass of water, but when she turned around again, he was washing them down with the beer.

He set the bottle on the table and began pulling his shirt on again. When she caught his eye, he said, "If you think I'm giving you another crack at my back, you're crazy."

"I wasn't about to touch your back again," she said, though the urge to do so was strong. "I was thinking about...going out on the balcony. The rain's letting up."

"Here," he said, standing. "I know just what you need." He picked up her glass of wine, pushed it into her hand, then opened the kitchen window a crack and set the radio close to it. "Come on," he said, taking her hand. "A rainy night and Dinah Washington. That should make you happy."

But she didn't know what would make her happy. She suspected it had something to do with Joe, and that scared her out of her wits. *Tell me about it, Dinah,* she thought as she followed him into the hall and out the door to the balcony. Dinah sang soulfully about the man she'd lost, and Lissa could feel the misery conveyed in the lyrics as though it was as tangible as the rain.

Two lawn chairs were folded against the wall, and Lissa opened them and pushed them back under the eaves. The rain was indeed lessening, and she turned up her face as a soft breeze blew some of the mist against her. Joe sat down heavily, and she didn't miss his wince. She twisted her wineglass in her hands, but didn't drink.

Somebody at the radio station was either a big Dinah Washington fan or else he'd gone to the bathroom and left the whole album to play. The music went on, sad and dreamy, and Lissa closed her eyes, leaning back against the wall.

"Did you like to go to dances when you were in school?" Joe asked at last.

"Dances?" Lissa repeated. She thought of how he'd held her close in the kitchen, and her blood heated. "No. I was tall and awkward. No boy wanted to dance with me."

"That's the trouble with boys," Joe said laconically. "They don't get any sense until they're thirty-five."

She was silent for a moment. "I guess that means you're sort of coming into your own right now."

He grinned, and she thought his eyes danced with devilment again, but it was too dark to tell. "Yeah, I've gained a little more knowledge about myself and life."

"Your son's a terrific kid," she told him. "Lots of common sense. He worries about you, doesn't he?"

"Yeah. All the time. He's ten going on thirty-five." He was quiet a moment, and she could feel him thinking about Jay. "He's had a rough time of it. Kind of caught between a rock and a hard place. It's not a pleasant place for a ten-year-old kid to be, but he . . . handles it."

Lissa took a deep breath and plunged ahead. "Your ex-wife? That's the rock and the hard place?"

"Yeah," he said quietly. "That's it. Caroline doesn't know what she wants, but whatever it is, she doesn't have it and she blames me. Does that make sense?"

"Yes, it makes a lot of sense," she said, understanding how hard it must be for Jay and how that must grieve Joe.

He took another swallow of beer, then abruptly set the bottle on the flooring and stood. He raked a hand through his hair and exhaled, a tight, pent-up sigh that spoke of building frustration. "I'm going . . . for a walk," he said without looking at her.

She didn't know what she'd done, what she'd said, unless it was the broaching of a forbidden topic—his ex-wife.

"Joe!" she said quickly, and he stopped. "I'm sorry. If you didn't want to talk about her, you could have just told me. I'd have understood."

He turned around slowly, and even in the dark she could make out the loneliness in his eyes. "It's not the conversation."

"Then what?" she demanded.

"Don't you know? I thought it was written all over my face." He gave her a wry smile, but the ache never left his eyes. "I can't sit here in the dark and talk and smell that sweet perfume you're wearing and not touch you. I want you, Lissa. I want you so much it hurts."

Seven

It still surprised her that he let her come with him.

He had asked Mrs. McGee to watch Jay and the baby, telling her that he and Lissa were going for a walk. With a hot, shuttered look at Lissa, a look that turned her knees to jelly, he'd grabbed his black leather jacket from the back of a chair in his apartment and propelled her into the hall. She crossed her arms over her white sweater and hurried to keep up with him, careful not to walk close enough beside him to accidentally touch.

It was almost June, but a cool front had stalled over the Mississippi River valley, and the air was chilly.

She remembered the night they'd walked to the coffee shop and the carefully controlled anger she'd felt in him then. Right now she felt another emotion, just as raw and urgent, but this time it was need.

A few drops of water dripped from the trees, pooling on the sidewalk and reflecting the cold moonlight. A chorus of frogs had taken up their song now that the rain was ended, but they sounded secretive and whispery to her tonight. On she walked beside Joe, glancing at his face from time to time and wondering what he was thinking.

She wasn't paying any attention to where they were going. She was too intent on her inner thoughts, on the battle that clamored inside her head. He hadn't asked her how she felt about the stark declaration that he wanted her; she hadn't volunteered to tell him.

She *did* want him. With all her being. And it scared the devil out of her, first because of Joe's warning that she should run away from him, and second because of the angry past they shared. She'd sworn she wouldn't be hurt by a man again, and here she was, falling in love with the man most capable of hurting her. *Falling in love.* Dear Lord, what was she getting herself into?

"Lissa, are you all right?" he asked, and she realized that they'd stopped walking. They were at the riverfront, the dark clouds once again partially obscuring the moon so that only a glimmer of light slithered across the water. A barge, its searchlight sweeping the dark, moved silently upriver, its wake slapping the shore in a slow rhythm,

"I'm...fine," she said, looking around. There were trailers and several pieces of machinery on the shore, their black hulks silvered by the moonlight. It was the first time she'd come face-to-face with Joe's work, and it impressed her. Where all this machinery stood, one day there would be a bridge. She knew what that would mean to the economy of the town.

"We're getting ready to cast the end approach sections," Joe said. "They'll be cast in place, but the ones nearest the river will have to be cast on the ground. We'll lift them into place with winches."

She didn't know anything about approach sections or casting, but she could clearly see that he knew a great deal.

He took his work seriously and it meant something to him. He was so different from his brother who'd cared nothing for work unless it was short and pleasant and paid extremely well.

"This is my office over here," he said, indicating a pale green trailer resting on concrete blocks. More blocks had been piled up to serve as stairs.

"Could I see it?"

He hesitated a second, and she felt him deciding whether to take her inside or not. "All right," he said finally, putting his hand on her shoulder to guide her. He unlocked the door, then reached down a hand to help her climb the concrete blocks. She told herself she knew what she was doing, asking to see the trailer, but in her heart she was still scared.

Joe flipped on a desk lamp and stood aside while she looked around. The desk dominated the trailer, and it appeared to be the center of activity. It was littered with piles of paper, drawings, pencils and several coffee-stained cups. A few packs of saltine crackers and an empty cardboard chili bowl from a local eatery lay on one corner.

"It's functional if not too attractive," Joe said as if reading her thoughts.

To the right of the desk was what must pass for a kitchen with a tiny, built-in refrigerator and a microwave oven. She thought there was a sink under the window, but the curtains were drawn, and it was so dark she couldn't be sure.

A plain brown couch sat against the dark back wall of the trailer. Like everything else in the trailer, the couch was the repository of stray items, in this case discarded newspapers and two empty potato chip bags. When Lissa looked back at Joe, he was watching her, his jaw tight. "Lissa—" he began. "We should go."

Slowly she shook her head. All she knew was that she needed him tonight. "We don't have to go, Joe. Not if you don't want to."

He didn't say anything for a moment, and when he spoke his voice was rough. "I don't want to."

Lissa didn't move, but Joe did. In one stride he was standing in front of her, and the next instant his hands slid beneath her cardigan and settled on her hips, pulling her closer to him.

"God, you smell so good," he murmured raggedly, surprised at his own thready pulse. This woman affected him like no other had. His mouth sought hers before she could frame a response, and she tasted as sweet as she smelled. He couldn't seem to hold onto his control when he was around her, and he didn't want to rush her.

But she was rushing, too, he decided, and the realization was not unpleasant. She was kissing him back as though she had been as frustrated as he. He could feel her urgency in the way she pressed her body against his.

He felt so right, she thought in distraction. So damn right when everything else told her that what she was doing was wrong.

He pulled off her cardigan there by the desk, and it joined the pile of papers. He was impatient, but he forced himself to slow down for her. His hands tugged up her turquoise blouse, fingers skimming her ribs and making her gasp softly. Her breasts were full and so incredibly soft that he groaned when his thumbs slid under her bra.

Impatience took over again, and Joe unhooked the lacy bra and pushed it up. He cupped her breasts, his thumbs stroking over the nipples until she was breathing as raggedly as he was. "You're so soft and beautiful," he murmured, lowering his mouth to her.

Hampered by her half-on, half-off clothing, Lissa began to unbutton her blouse but stopped on an aching sigh when Joe's tongue touched her nipple. She was trembling under his mouth, and she swayed against him, rocked with desire.

Joe still couldn't believe that she wanted this, wanted *him*, and he drew back slightly to look at her. She was so incredibly beautiful. Her eyes were closed, her mouth slightly open in pleasure. For a painful instant the dread crossed his mind that she was thinking about Alex even as he touched her, but he wouldn't let himself believe that. He wanted Lissa, but he wasn't going to play stand-in for his dead brother.

"Look at me," he whispered, drawing a finger gently down her cheek. "Tell me what you see."

Slowly her eyes opened, studying him through a glaze of need. Her hands rested on his shoulders, the tightness of her grip testament to the force of that need.

Lissa knew he wasn't asking for a physical assessment, though she could have given him a pretty flattering one. He was lean and tall and tightly muscled, and she loved the sight of him. But he was also gentle and caring, though he would have denied the latter, and his dark brown eyes were filled with raw desire.

"I see a man I respect, a man who cares very much for his son and for his friends," she said softly. "I see a man who works very hard and honors his commitments." Her voice shook slightly. "I want you, Joe." There was no way she could ever want Alex now. She had meant everything she'd said about Joe. He was honest and decent, and he made her blood sing.

He scooped her up so quickly that it made her breath catch. At the couch he set her down, then swept the clutter onto the floor. "Let me undress you," he whispered urgently, sitting beside her and pulling off her blouse and bra. She kicked away her shoes, and Joe unfastened her jeans, tugging them down while she lifted her hips to help him. Her panties came away with the jeans and ended up on the floor with the rest of her clothes.

Joe ran his hand over her thighs, making her shiver in anticipation. Then he slowly stood and began pulling off his leather jacket and T-shirt. His eyes were riveted to her as he unfastened his jeans and kicked off his shoes.

She needed to touch him, to see him, to taste him.

"I want to see you," she whispered, reaching over to turn on the lamp on the end table.

She could have sworn he was embarrassed when she saw the expression in his eyes, and it only endeared him to her more.

"I don't have a pretty body," he told her. "I've got calluses and more than my share of scars."

But Lissa wanted Joe to know how beautiful he was to her.

She looked at him in the lamplight, then reached out and finished undressing him, dropping his jeans and undershorts to the floor. He was right—he was hard and callused, and a few thin scars bore testament to old injuries. But he was Joe. "Do you know," she said, "that you are the handsomest man I've ever seen?"

It was clear he didn't believe her, but he was flattered anyway.

"I mean it," she said when he raised his brows and grinned at her.

His grin widened. "I think you're giving me the business, but I'm just old enough and worked up enough to like it."

She had to laugh at that. But he was indeed "worked up enough" and he proved that by picking her up again and holding her on his lap. She could feel his arousal pressing against her thigh, and she reached down with her hands to stroke him.

He inhaled sharply and nuzzled her neck. "You drive me crazy, do you know that?" he murmured.

"I mean to," she said truthfully. She set about kissing him, and he leaned back against the couch, pulling her down on top of his chest.

"Let's go slow," he suggested, but his hands and mouth belied his words. He was touching her all over, making her hot and cold at the same time with the tender coaxing of his fingers and lips. Her breasts were nestled against the thick mat of his chest hair, and he reached his fingers beneath them to stroke her there. She levered herself up, straddling him, and Joe molded his mouth around one breast, his tongue deliciously teasing the nipple until she cried out his name.

Again she reached down for him, stroking with her hands, and he groaned. "Yes, honey. Oh, yes."

But he wouldn't let her do that for long. He had her on her back the next instant, and he was lying over her, his right foot on the floor because the couch was too narrow. Joe caressed her between her thighs, making her arch against his hand as her breathing became more erratic. She loved the touch of his hard hands, his fingers so strong and rough-textured, yet so gentle with her. He was clearly intent on giving her as much pleasure as he could, but she wanted to pleasure him, too, and she wanted him deep inside her.

"Joe," she urged him, parting her legs even more. "I want you."

"Lissa, honey, this isn't going slow," he told her hoarsely.

"No, it isn't," she assured him. "I don't want slow."

Without further preliminaries, Joe entered her, and though she knew he was trying to be more deliberate even now, he wasn't succeeding. He held perfectly still for a moment, and she searched his eyes. What she saw there was an honesty that almost made her flinch.

"I never wanted to *want* you this badly," he told her. "I never wanted to need anyone like this, least of all you. But I do, and I can't help myself. I don't want to hurt you anymore than I already have."

It still didn't rest easy with him, the need he felt around Lissa, the way his body demanded her, the way his mind constantly sought her image. It was so hard for him to admit to that need, but she understood because it was hard for her, too.

"I never admired the way my brother lived his life," he said as if this was something he had to tell her before he could make love to her. "But I didn't want to believe the worst of him, either. I was . . . angry after you told me he'd lied to you. I didn't want to give up my memory of who—and what—Alex was." His hand shook slightly as he traced a gentle path down her cheek. "I won't believe he was totally bad," he told her with unflinching honesty. "I'll never believe that."

"I know," she whispered, touching his lips with two fingers. "I know."

Joe gave her everything he could then, gave her all that his body and heart were capable of giving, and Lissa clutched at him, trying to remember not to touch his back where he was bruised. She clung to his shoulders until she felt the tension pour from him as he cried out her name. A second later she was arching against him, biting back the words of love that welled in her throat.

The only way they could both lie on the couch was with Lissa's back against Joe's chest and one of Joe's legs thrown over her. They managed to settle in that position in the long, drowsy afterglow, Joe's fingers lightly stroking Lissa's breast.

"Best work I've ever done in this trailer," he said with obvious satisfaction, and Lissa smiled in the dark. He'd turned off the lamp before settling his arms around her, and she marveled at how much she loved lying here in the dark with him.

"Are you fishing for compliments, Joe?" she teased him.

"Yeah," he admitted. "I was hoping you'd give me the business again about how handsome I am."

That made her smile widen, but she obliged him, praising him until she was sure he was practically glowing with male satisfaction. It was his turn then, and he told her how beautiful she was, told her so quietly and gently that she believed every word and ached for more. When she turned as best she could in the close confinement of the couch, he began kissing her, and she could feel his rising desire. It was the same for her, the same swift climb to heat and need, and they moved together in the dark.

When he held her afterward, she felt the first stirrings of anxiety over what she'd done. It hit her with stunning force that she'd just made love to the man who'd threatened to take away her child. Her heart believed he could never do that to her, but a voice inside her head argued that he'd as much as told her he was capable of anything. She felt sadness creeping in where passion had burned.

Joe must have sensed her withdrawal or she may have involuntarily stiffened, because he said, "What's wrong?"

"Nothing," she told him, stroking his hair to make him believe her. She could feel him worrying in the dark, and she knew he was going to ask again. "We ought to get back to the children," she said quietly, disengaging herself from his arms and bending down to pick up her clothes. He didn't say anything, but she could feel the question he wasn't asking. *How are things between us now?* But she didn't know.

They didn't speak on the walk back to the apartment. Lissa hugged her arms to herself, and though Joe put his arm around her shoulder and drew her close, she didn't lean on him. When he held her and gave her a light kiss on her forehead, she stood still but made no move to touch him. Joe gave her a long, searching look, then left without another word.

Lissa slept fitfully that night, and the next morning she got out of bed early and sat at the kitchen table, studying for finals in both history and English lit. She couldn't seem to concentrate; Black Jack Pershing and Lord Byron became hopelessly entangled.

Lissa knew she was in love with Joe; it was futile to pretend otherwise after last night. Everything had happened so fast with him, and yet she knew that what she felt was real. She sat at the table in her short blue nightgown and summoned up images of Joe kissing her, Joe making slow, exquisite love to her. She wasn't the kind of woman who gave of herself lightly. She was a big girl, and she'd known what she was getting into when she went to bed with him. But risking her own future was far different than risking that of her daughter. *I trust him,* she told herself.

"Lissa?"

She jumped when she heard Joe's voice. When she looked up, she saw him standing hesitantly just inside the door.

"I tapped on the door," he said, "but I guess you didn't hear me."

"I'm studying," she said with a wry smile, indicating the books in front of her. "Finals."

"I won't keep you then. I just wanted you to know that I have to go out of town for a few days to meet with our concrete supplier. I'm taking Jay with me."

"Oh." She stared back at him, feeling an emptiness inside before he was even gone.

Joe watched the expression change on her face, then held out a hand. "Come here," he said quietly.

She stood and went willingly into his arms. They were warm, strong arms, and they enfolded her tightly, held her to him so close that she could hear the steady cadence of his heart.

"Will you miss me?" he whispered.

"I'll miss your beef Burgundy," she teased him.

"I'm part of the package deal," he informed her. "Miss my beef, miss me."

"All right," she said agreeably, smiling into his chest. Her hand idly plucked at the back of his shirt as she wished she could undress him right here and now. Her smile widened as she thought of big, brash Joe Douglas with all his arrogant bossiness letting her undress him. She decided she really enjoyed teasing him. "You know," she said, "I could put up one of those hanging pot racks for you. Don't you French chefs like your pots hanging out for all the world to see?"

"I'm not hanging anything out for anyone to see," he growled into her hair. "Besides, your place is too small and you're not going to be here that much longer."

It took a minute for his words to register, and when they did, her laughter fled. Slowly she drew back from him and raised questioning eyes to his face. "What?" she said.

The tightening of his jaw told her he expected a fight on this. "You're moving into new quarters, sweetheart," he informed her. "I found a little house five blocks over that's ideal. It has three bedrooms, so Suzanne will have her own room. And there's a nice big backyard for her to play in. You can take a look at it when you want and decide what colors you want for the interior." Determined brown eyes dared her to object.

Lissa shook off his hands that still held her and stepped farther away from him. He could have stopped her from withdrawing, but he made no move to keep her near him. "How dare you!"

"Look, I expected you to be upset—"

"Upset?" she repeated angrily. "Try infuriated. How could you just assume that I'd pack up and go where you want me to go? I have no intention of leaving this apartment! For one thing, I can't afford anything else."

"You aren't going to be paying for it," he informed her, planting his hands on his hips.

"Do you really think you can just order me to live where you want me to live?" she demanded, her voice rising. She threw up her hands in a gesture of supreme impatience. "I'm already driving the car you want me to drive. And using the diaper service you arranged. Maybe you'd like to pick out my clothes while you're at it," she finished sarcastically.

His eyes took on a seductive gleam, tempered by his anger, as he looked her up and down. "Yeah, maybe I would," he said softly.

"Well, forget it!" she snapped. "And you can forget about my moving. I'm not the least bit interested."

"Then you'd better generate a little interest, honey," he advised her stonily. "You're being evicted."

"What?" She couldn't have been more surprised had he told her that she was sprouting wings.

"Mrs. McGee is going to turn the downstairs into a small shop. She'll live upstairs in one apartment, and one of her sisters is going to live in the other."

"She told you this?" Lissa demanded skeptically.

Joe shrugged. "I sort of suggested it."

"And you probably told her that I was thrilled with the whole thing." She crossed her arms and glared at him. The man was insufferable.

"I said you wouldn't object," he admitted.

"Well, I do object."

"Too bad," he said, blithely dismissing her argument. "I want you and the baby in a nicer home."

"That's so generous," she said in carefully spaced acid tones. "And what do you get out of this?" Her eyebrows arched.

Joe looked at the floor. "After last night, I thought I might spend the night there with you on occasion."

"Guess again," she snapped. "I'm not your mistress, and I have no intention of becoming one. You can take your tidy little arrangement and stuff it!"

"Lissa!" His voice demanded attention, but she was already turning away from him, knotting her hands at her sides as if that could stifle the fury that was boiling inside her. "Look at me," he insisted, one hand closing on her shoulder and making her face him again. "We're doing this my way."

"Sorry, but I won't cooperate," she told him from between gritted teeth. "I won't let you dictate how I live my life. I have to draw the line somewhere, and this is where I'm doing it. I'm not moving. You can't buy me."

He watched her in a long moment of silence, and she could feel him restraining his own temper. That was almost more frightening than if he'd yelled at her. His eyes, so stormy a moment ago, darkened to glittering obsidian. His fingers on her shoulder tightened fractionally, and still she faced him down.

"Are you sure you don't want to reconsider?" he asked, his voice nearly a whisper. "In your own interests?"

"Are you threatening me?" she asked, trying to keep her voice steady. Lissa could feel her heart pounding with so much force that she was nearly breathless. She had to make him understand that he couldn't intimidate her into doing everything he wanted. She had to stand her ground now—and take the consequences if need be. She was in love with the man, but she couldn't sacrifice all her independence to him.

His hand slowly left her shoulder and gently cupped her cheek. "Does this feel like a threat?" he murmured, tilting her chin up. His eyes probed hers for what seemed an eternity before his mouth softly brushed hers. She could feel his own frustration as clearly as her own.

He gave her one more tantalizing, brief kiss and then he walked out the door, leaving her staring after him.

Ten minutes later she heard him going down the stairs with his son, Jay chattering and Joe silent.

When Lissa returned from class that night and picked up Suzanne at Mrs. McGee's apartment, the landlady said, "I've got something for you."

She gave Lissa a significant look as she handed her a plastic shopping bag.

"What is it?"

Mrs. McGee raised her brows. "I think you ought to see for yourself. It's not my place to go telling someone what someone else got them for a present."

Mystified, Lissa reached into the bag and pulled out an album, a Dinah Washington album. For a minute she couldn't say anything for her overwhelming sense of misery and loss.

"Don't you want to know who gave it to you?" Mrs. McGee asked curiously.

But Lissa knew. It was Joe. "Did he say anything?" she asked, wanting some small piece of him, any tidbit that Mrs. McGee could give her.

"Well, not that I can recollect," Mrs. McGee said thoughtfully. "Other than I should give this to you. He dropped by with Jay before they left this morning." The unspoken question must have been written all over Lissa's face, because Mrs. McGee studied her with a frown and said, "He looked tired. And mad. Mad as hell. Would you know anything about who put him in that frame of mind?"

"I did," Lissa admitted. She wanted to see him again, so she could kiss that smug look from his face and wring his neck—and she wasn't sure which she'd do first.

"Well, those things happen when you're young," Mrs. McGee said philosophically. "Happen when you're old, too, but by then you're too ornery to worry about it. Offhand, I'd say you're worrying about it, aren't you?"

"A little," she said reluctantly. She was lying; she was worrying about it a lot.

"If you take my advice," Mrs. McGee said, her tone implying that one would be a fool not to, "you'll find yourself a nice broken clock and fix the heck out of it. You'll forget your worries in nothing flat."

Lissa had to smile at Mrs. McGee's remedy. If everyone took Mrs. McGee's advice, there wouldn't be a soul in the world who knew the correct time.

"Did you hear about my shop?" Mrs. McGee asked, her eyes lighting up.

"Yes. Joe told me about it. Congratulations."

Mrs. McGee beamed. "Thank you, dear. But I couldn't manage it without Joe. He's going to do the remodeling for next to nothing. And he's going to invest, so I can get my start-up inventory." She leaned toward Lissa with a conspiratorial smile. "Small appliances. My specialty."

"That sounds very nice," Lissa said politely.

"I'm really sorry to lose you as a tenant, but Joe said you and the baby need a larger home and he's right."

Lissa bit back her retort that Joe only *thought* he was right. But she realized that Mrs. McGee was truly excited about the shop. She thanked her and took her record and her baby upstairs, playing Dinah Washington while she fixed some supper.

She was playing the record again Friday night when she heard Joe's truck stop behind the apartment and then two sets of footsteps climb the stairs. It was a hot, muggy night, and she had the windows open, so he must have heard the music drifting out, but he didn't stop at her door. She heard Jay ask something, but she couldn't make out what it was or what Joe answered.

She had trusted him enough to stand up to him, and now all she could do was wait to see what he would do. She lay awake a long time that night, getting up twice to soothe Suzanne whose gums were bothering her. She was bone-tired when the phone rang at seven a.m.

It was a crisis of major proportions with Bonnie Ann, the only kind of crisis that Bonnie Ann ever had.

"You've *got* to help me!" Bonnie Ann implored. "I don't have anyone else to ask. Honest!"

"Help you what?" Lissa said.

"Get my driver's license!"

It turned out that the person who wrote the book on efficiency, the person who juggled twenty-three projects in the air at the same time, had just dropped one on her head. Bonnie Ann had somehow let her driver's license lapse. And now she needed Lissa to take her to the examining station so she could take the test. Before noon.

Joe was driving back to the apartment with groceries, worried because he could see that something was on Jay's mind.

"Did you and Lissa have a fight, Dad?" Jay asked at last.

Joe shook his head, wondering how to explain to Jay how it was sometimes between a man and a woman. "There are things we need to sort out," he said at last. "Problems."

Jay thought about that a minute. "If you get married to Lissa, Dad...will you and her start yelling at each other like you and Mom yell at each other?"

Joe tightened his grip on the steering wheel, feeling a stab of pain for what his son had gone through, was still enduring. He checked the rearview mirror, then pulled the truck to the side of the road.

"Jay, Lissa and I are trying to work things out without yelling at each other. Well, not too much, anyway. What happened between your mom and me isn't the same. Your mom is unhappy, and that makes her yell. Some people yell when they're unhappy and some cry."

"Yeah," Jay agreed. "I used to cry a lot."

Joe put his arm around his son's shoulder, pulling him toward him. "Listen, Jay, if you ever feel like crying again or if things just get rough...you come tell me, okay?"

"Okay," Jay said quietly.

"There's one other thing," Joe said, deciding this was something Jay needed to know.

"What?"

"You know Lissa's baby...Suzanne?"

"Yeah." Jay smiled; he was fond of the baby.

"Suzanne's father was your uncle Alex. Suzanne's your cousin." He waited to see how Jay would digest this.

Jay thought that bit of information over a bit. "Does that mean you can't marry Lissa?" he asked at last. "Is she my aunt?"

Joe shook his head. "No. It just means that things are a little more complicated. It's part of what Lissa and I have to work out." He took a deep breath.

"You know, Dad," Jay said philosophically, "you've got a...what do you call it?...an interesting life."

"Ain't it the truth," Joe agreed, ruffling Jay's hair.

The phone was ringing when they walked in the apartment.

"Joe?" Bonnie Ann's obvious distress was making her voice quiver. "It's me...Bonnie Ann...from Duncans' Quik Stop. Oh, Joe, I'm here with Lissa at the hospital."

He felt his heart lurch upward. "What happened, Bonnie Ann?" he demanded.

"A truck ran a stop sign... It hit us broadside. Lissa's arm's broken."

Eight

It was Joe who took her home from the hospital, Joe who assured Bonnie Ann that the accident wasn't her fault and she should stop berating herself, that no, the driver's license bureau wasn't going to confiscate her new license. It was Joe who made sure he had all of Lissa's belongings and Joe who gingerly helped her into the truck. Mrs. McGee watched the children until Lissa was comfortably settled.

Back in her apartment, Joe insisted that she lie down on her bed, and, lulled by the painkiller, Lissa drifted off to sleep. She awoke later to the sound of Joe's voice in the kitchen. She couldn't hear anyone answer him, only his voice followed by tense pauses, and she realized he was on the telephone. The room was partially in darkness, and she decided it was early evening.

"What do you mean you're too busy for him?" he was saying angrily. His voice was level, but Lissa sensed he was being pushed to the limit by someone. *Caroline,* an inner voice told her. "What's your excuse this time? Too many parties lined up or do you have a new boyfriend who doesn't want your son hanging around and spoiling his time in the sack with you?" The last was said in a deliberately sarcastic, cutting voice.

Another long, exasperated pause, punctuated by a sharp exhalation. Lissa slowly got off the bed, holding her arm gingerly, and padded to the doorway in her socks. The baby was lying in her infant carrier, absorbed in a rubber duck squeeze toy, her attention occasionally diverted to Joe who was pacing the kitchen like a caged animal, the telephone cord his leash. His eyes were fixed on the floor, and he didn't see Lissa, but his agitation was apparent. He shoved one hand forcefully through his hair.

"Look, you don't want to see your son, then you tell him yourself. Don't expect me to be the one to let him know his mother doesn't give a damn about him." He grunted harshly. "Yeah, well, you go have a good time," he said coldly. "Just remember when you go looking for my check in the mailbox that it may not be there if you don't give your son a little time and attention."

She must have hung up on him, because Joe cursed softly, then tossed the receiver back on the hook. He stood for a moment with his back to her, his hands on his hips, and then he turned as if he'd sensed her presence.

"I'm sorry I woke you," he said gruffly, but his eyes softened. "Jay told me his mom called and wanted to talk to me."

"It's all right. Is she . . . giving you trouble about Jay?" She didn't know if she had the right to ask him that, but she wanted to know. What happened to both him and Jay was important to her.

"Yeah." He came to her and reached out to stroke back some hair from her cheek. His touch felt so good that she wanted to lean against him, but she sensed some reserve in him. "She's supposed to have Jay next week, but she can't seem to clear her schedule for him."

"Can't you do anything? Compromise with her?"

Joe snorted. "Compromise is an alien concept to Caroline," he said. "The only thing she understands is the alimony check I send every month. If the check's late, she's a bit more amenable to reason."

"Can't she get the court on you if the check's late?" Lissa asked.

"She could," Joe admitted, a certain amount of grim satisfaction creeping into his eyes. "But she knows I could cause her a great deal of trouble in turn if I wanted. She's tangled with me in court before."

Lissa remembered what Bonnie Ann had told her, and she suppressed a shiver. She could believe that Joe was totally ruthless were it not for the gentleness she could see in the depths of his eyes, the gentleness she'd experienced.

"What is it?" he asked her softly, his hand touching her cheek again. "Your arm's hurting," he said before she could answer. "Come lie down again."

He led her back to the bedroom and settled her on top of the comforter, pulling an afghan over her. He eased himself onto the edge of the bed, his hip touching hers through the afghan. "Are you tired?" he asked.

She shook her head. "Worried, I suppose."

"What are you worried about?"

"You," she said candidly, meeting his eyes.

"Are you afraid of me?" he asked, and she could see the concern in his face.

"No, I don't think so," she said, allowing him a small smile.

"Apparently not," he said wryly. "Considering how you stood up to me a couple of days ago." He caressed her hand lightly with his thumb, his eyes smoky with longing as he watched her. "I don't want you to be afraid of me, Lissa. It

drives me crazy when you insist on doing whatever it is you
want to do, no matter that I can give you something better.
But—'' He shot her a frustrated, heated look laced with
humor. ''But you're a strong woman, honey, and I'd rather
fight with you any day than be with a dozen other women
who kowtow to every one of my whims.''

''Well, you came to the right place, fella,'' she advised
him as cockily as she could while still under the influence of
painkillers.

''Lissa,'' he said, turning serious again. ''I've told you
that I do whatever's necessary when I'm pushed. With-
holding Caroline's money is small potatoes compared to
other things I've done.'' He paused. ''After my little girl
died, I went to court to get custody of Jay. I got the tough-
est lawyer I could find, and I threatened Caroline with every
trick in the book, foremost being a cutoff of money from
me.'' His touch was silk, but his eyes were steel. ''She caved
in, and I got Jay.''

''I know,'' she said quietly. ''Bonnie Ann told me.''

''Bonnie Ann?'' He looked surprised.

''She has a cousin who lives near you. She knew the whole
story.''

''It's a small town,'' he said wryly. ''Not many secrets.''

''No, I suppose not.'' She felt a sense of relief that he'd
told her himself.

The baby gave a whimper from the kitchen, and Joe
gently restrained Lissa when she moved to get up. ''I'll get
her,'' he said. ''I think I'll start dinner, too. Can you eat
something?''

''If you're cooking—yes.''

He grinned and bent to brush her mouth with his before
he levered himself from the bed. She lay there listening to
him soothe the baby and move about the kitchen, rattling
pots and pans. She hadn't wanted Bonnie Ann to call Joe

from the hospital, but there was no stopping Bonnie Ann
when she was on a runaway guilt trip.

Lissa was afraid that Joe wouldn't come, that after their
latest disagreement he would turn his back on her at the
least. Other people in her life had in the past. But he hadn't.
And she marveled again at how much she was trusting him,
how much of her protective guard she'd let down for him.

She understood why he had a ruthless streak. Hell, she'd
have done the same thing if it were Suzanne at stake. She
also understood why he carried a basic mistrust of women.
His ex-wife had pulled enough tricks to jade even Phil
Donahue. But deep down Lissa sensed that Joe was the man
she'd waited for all her life. Beneath the gruffness and the
arrogance was the man who'd immediately come to the
hospital without question to get her, the man who cooked
her spectacular dinners and the man who made her body
sing when he touched her. If she was right about the man,
then she'd found a heaven and a haven. If she was wrong...

She didn't even want to contemplate what kind of hell
that would be.

Lissa must have drifted off to sleep again, because she
awoke a while later to a tantalizing aroma emanating from
the kitchen and the low exchange of male voices.

"I'm really sorry about it, son," Joe was saying, "but
your mom's tied up with some other things right now, and
she's afraid that if you came to see her right now, she
wouldn't be able to spend much time with you. Maybe next
month."

There was a silence, then Jay's subdued voice. "She didn't
want me to come, did she, Dad?"

"Jay, I'm sure it wasn't that. Your mother loves you. It's
just that she . . . gets caught up in other things sometimes."
Lissa had a vivid image of Joe's hands resting on Jay's
shoulders, comforting his son as best he could. She remembered waking before to the sound of Joe on the phone with

Caroline and his barely controlled anger at her lack of interest in her son. Despite his claims to ruthlessness, he wasn't tarring Caroline with her own neglect in front of his son.

"Yeah, well, *you* always have time," Jay said, the resentment still in his voice.

She could feel Joe's heavy sigh. "Believe me, son, a lot of times I don't do as well as I should. But we'll make the best of this, won't we?"

"Okay," Jay said reluctantly. "Hey, Dad, maybe me and you could take Lissa back home when I go to the birthday party. I bet she'd love our house."

"We'll see," Joe said. "Dinner's almost ready. Come on. You set the table, and I'll wake her up."

Lissa pretended to be asleep when Joe came into the bedroom, and she stretched lazily as he sat on the bed.

"Mmm, smells delicious out there," she murmured.

"The chef lives only for your approval," he said.

"Yeah, right."

Joe grinned at that and gently ruffled her hair. "Come on, sassy," he told her. "I'm starving." The look he gave her indicated he was starving for more than food at the moment, and she felt her heart take up its familiar unruly cadence at his meaning. Briefly he kissed her forehead, then led her to the kitchen.

It was another delicious meal, though Joe assured her it was simple to prepare, a favorite of his mother's. The custardy ham and leek dish was a *clafouti*, he said, traditionally a fruit dessert but easily improvised into a main dish. With it he'd fixed a salad with walnut dressing and crusty rolls. Because of the medication she was on, Joe fixed Lissa tea instead of wine.

Suzanne held out her arms from her infant seat, insisting that Joe hold her. He balanced her on his lap while he ate, feeding her cereal and strained apricots from a baby plate next to his own plate. Her completely happy, burbling baby made Lissa realize how easily Joe had settled himself in her life.

"I'm totally spoiled now," Lissa assured him when she'd finished her meal and repeatedly murmured her enthusiastic approval. "I have two choices. Either I can hire you, which necessitates some expenditure, or I can kidnap you and make you cook like this every day, and since I don't have any money to speak of..." She shrugged her shoulders in a parody of resignation.

"You sweet-talker you," he said, raising his brows and giving her a suggestive smile that sent her pulse thudding off the Richter scale. "You really know the way to a man's...heart."

"It's a gift," she told him, waggling her brows at him and making him laugh.

"What are you guys talking about?" Jay asked curiously, his chin in his hand as he eyed first one, then the other.

"Isn't it your bedtime?" Joe asked, leaning back and regarding his son.

"Dad, it's only nine o'clock," Jay protested. "What, I ask one question and I have to go to bed?"

Joe raised an eyebrow, and Jay sighed. "Can I read in bed?" he bargained.

"Yeah. I'll check on you later."

When Jay had left, Joe stood and stretched and set Suzanne in her carrier. "Time to get you ready for bed, too."

"Me?" Lissa said, startled. "I think I'll stay up a while." After her long nap and the teasing conversation with Joe, she couldn't possibly sleep.

"Stay up as long as you want, but I'm getting you ready for bed." Taking in what must have been her incredulous expression, Joe said, "If you think you can undress all by yourself with that cast on your arm, you'd better think again.''

He was right, of course, and she realized it as soon as he began to undress her in her bedroom. She had only the use of her left arm, and she had no dexterity. Putting up with him undressing her was another matter though. It made her feel not only helpless, but helplessly aroused. His fingers brushed her lightly as he peeled off her jeans, and her legs tingled and her knees grew weak.

Joe was still making an effort not to look at her face, but when he began gently pulling off her top, his eyes met hers. She saw the tension there before he looked away.

She started to say his name, but he began talking, a move she suspected was calculated to distract her.

''We'll get this over your left arm first,'' he said, ''then your head. We'll slip it over the cast last.''

He busied himself talking her through her disrobing, instructing her to put her arm or her leg here or there, until she stood before him in only panties and bra. ''Joe,'' she said softly, but he was still intent on putting her off.

He was rummaging through her drawers until he came up with a nightshirt. ''Okay?'' he asked, holding up a pink one with a lace collar.

''It's fine, but—''

''Here, let's get it over your head.'' Any communication was effectively cut off again as he slid the shift over her head. From the back he unhooked her bra and pushed it off her shoulders. Lissa let it slide down her arms and onto the floor. Joe worked gently to maneuver her cast through the short sleeve of the nightshirt and then she felt his hands fall away.

''Can you get into bed by yourself?''

''Yes, of course, but, Joe—'' She turned around to face him and broke off when she saw the stubborn set to his face. Lissa sighed. There was so much intensity in their relation-

ship that both fought with uncompromising determination
not to give an inch. "Joe, thank you for doing all of this.
I—"

"No thanks are necessary," he broke in, sounding chid-
ing. "You know I'll do whatever I can for you and Suzanne."

She knew that. She also knew that it wasn't enough. She
wanted all of Joe Douglas, and he was still obstinately
keeping some part of himself from her. She wanted him
teasing and laughing as he'd been at dinner. She knew intimacy threatened him, and she knew why, but that knowledge didn't diminish her frustration.

"Listen, honey, we need to get a couple of things
straightened out." She knew from the obstinate look on his
face that she wasn't going to like what he had to say next.
"I'm going to take care of you. I promise you that. But
maybe the other night was . . . a mistake. Maybe we should
have done a little more thinking before we let things get out
of hand." Dammit, she was overcome again with that irresistible urge to choke Joe.

"A mistake," she repeated. "Joe, I know what you're
doing, and I don't buy it. You don't want emotional involvement, and I can understand why you feel that way. But
I think you're already emotionally involved, and you just
won't admit it to yourself—or me."

"Is that what you think?" he demanded harshly.
Abruptly he bent to turn out the small bedside lamp, but
before the room was plunged into darkness, Lissa had seen
the torment burning in his eyes.

"Yes," she whispered shakily. "That's what I think. I
think you're afraid of your own feelings, of being hurt
again."

"That's a strange sentiment coming from the woman who
raised the roof when I wanted to move her to a house." His

tone was even, and she couldn't determine what he was thinking.

"That was another one of your plans to have things your own way without any commitment," she told him, determined not to back down. "You wanted to set me up in a house and come and go as you pleased with me there at your beck and call."

"That wasn't it," he said, his voice low and vibrant.

"No?"

He didn't say anything, and the silence lengthened between them. From the bed Lissa could see the shadows from the bedroom encroaching into the dimly lighted kitchen. She could hear Suzanne babbling softly in her carrier and the overwrought ticking of the cat clock. Sounds of home. They made her heart clench as she thought of Joe turning his back on those things.

"I'd better put the baby to bed," he said at last, his voice strained. "I'll sleep on the couch tonight in case she wakes up. I'm going to lock the back door and leave open the doors to your apartment and mine, so I can hear Jay, too." Her eyes were adjusting to the dark, and she saw his silhouette move toward the door and into the light spilling from the kitchen. He looked tired and edgy. "Try to get some rest," he told her before he shut the door to her bedroom.

He was back later with Suzanne, tiptoeing in and laying her in her crib in the alcove. Lissa lay perfectly still, unable to sleep but not wanting him to know. Her muscles were stiff and sore from the accident and her arm ached, but her heart hurt even more.

She must have finally slept because the next thing she knew there was light in her eyes and someone was standing by the bed. "Joe?" she murmured before she opened her eyes.

"Yeah, it's me, baby. Did you get enough sleep?" He sat down on the edge of the bed, and she saw that he looked as ragged as she felt. He stroked back her hair and managed a gaunt smile. "Here, I brought you some coffee."

She took the coffee gratefully, but her eyes never left his. "I didn't sleep very well," she admitted. "I kept thinking of you on the couch."

Joe slowly rubbed the back of his neck. "Yeah, I didn't get much rest, either." He dropped his eyes from hers, stretching his back. "Come on," he said, his features tight. "Let's get you dressed."

He kept his eyes averted as he stood, and Lissa saw his discomfort in his tense shoulders and the impatient gesture of jamming his hands in his pockets. Her eyes lowered to his jeans, and his discomfort became more evident.

"Will this do?" he asked, rummaging in her closet and holding out a red blouse with roomy short sleeves and a pair of white slacks.

"Fine," she demurred, sliding out of bed. She was still stiff, and she steadied herself by leaning on the night table.

He was in even more discomfort when he opened her underwear drawer. She saw his mouth tighten as he pulled out a blue teddy with tiny buttons and quickly tossed it back into the drawer. Gritting his teeth, he hauled out a pair of lacy pink panties and a matching bra.

Joe still wouldn't meet her eyes when he stood before her with the underwear. He began gently pulling off her nightgown, and she heard a ragged breath escape his throat when the gown had cleared her waist and breasts and was wadded around her neck. He worked as quickly as he could, but he seemed to be all thumbs, and he swore softly.

Lissa stood looking back at him, clad only in panties, as the gown landed on the floor. Joe still wouldn't look at her. "Can you get those off by yourself?" he ground out, giving a cursory nod toward the skimpy slip of fabric she was wearing.

"Yes," she murmured. "I think so." She managed to peel off the panties one-handed, but she knew she couldn't put on clean underwear by herself. And there was something else. "Joe," she said hesitantly.

"What?"

"I need a shower."

He groaned.

A shower was impractical with the cast, so Joe ran a tub of warm water for her and helped her inside. His jaw was clenched, his brows a dark straight slash as he handed her a washcloth. "Can you manage this without help?"

She could, except for her back, and she called out to him when she was about done. He came back into the bathroom soundlessly, his expression still one of the tormented stoic, and Lissa gestured toward her back with the washcloth. "If you don't mind," she said tentatively. "I can't reach."

Wordlessly he took the cloth and knelt by the tub. What followed was a slow, gentle rubbing of her back that had her alternately purring in contentment and gnashing her teeth in frustration. She wished he'd pull her into his arms and kiss the living daylights out of her. But she knew he wouldn't. Joe had been rocked back on his heels by her assertion that he cared about her but was afraid to admit it. Afraid intimacy might jar loose the feelings he was hiding inside, he was doing his damnedest to avoid touching her.

Lissa knew what he was going through. But understanding didn't salve her own need as he finished scrubbing her back and helped her to her feet, wrapping her in a large bath towel.

"Stand still," he ordered, hastily patting her dry, then holding out the clean panties. "All right. Left leg up." She complied with his directions, and he slid the panties up her legs and over her hips, his scowl deepening. The bra proved more difficult, but he made her turn around while he worked from the back. Still, she couldn't help noticing that his fingers were trembling as he slipped it over her breasts, and she felt his sharp exhalation against her back as he fastened the clasp.

Her flesh seemed to be on fire from head to toe, and she didn't think she could stand much more of his personal ministrations. She stood quietly as he helped her on with the blouse and slacks and then the shoes.

"I'll see if the baby's up," he ground out, turning on his heel and stalking from the bathroom.

He was in a bearish mood the rest of the day, and so was she.

Bonnie Ann had the bad timing to show up right after lunch, offering her heartfelt apologies for the accident and playing the role of Patron Saint of Guilt to the hilt. She offered to bring over casseroles and was taken aback when Lissa explained that Joe was not only an adequate cook but an excellent one.

Then she offered to do Lissa's laundry, but Joe told her he could do it himself. Lissa walked Bonnie Ann back out to her car, assuring her every step of the way that the accident wasn't her fault.

"Is he for real?" Bonnie Ann breathed, nodding toward the apartment.

"A little too real sometimes," Lissa admitted.

"Marry him," Bonnie Ann advised.

"There's one little hitch," Lissa said. "He hasn't asked me."

"Well, he'll get around to it," Bonnie Ann assured her as she hopped into her car. "Any guy who'd take care of you the way he is has to get around to marriage sooner or later."

But Lissa wasn't so sure. She didn't even know how deep Joe's feelings ran. She had to admit to herself that she didn't even know if they were genuine feelings. She'd called his bluff about his vulnerability, but all she had to go on was a hunch and an ache in her heart whenever she looked at him.

He'd thrown the laundry into the washer when she got back upstairs and now he was heading out the door.

"Jay's at a friend's house and I'm going for a walk," he said tersely.

"Can I come with you?" she asked, throwing caution to the wind.

"Sure, why not?"

Joe carried Suzanne, who was entranced with everything she saw, pointing her chubby finger here and there. Joe obliged her, stopping and kneeling while she reached for a dandelion poking through a crack in the sidewalk, and later tickling her chin with a blade of new grass until she giggled and kicked her legs.

The day was warm and sunny, the air heavy with the sound of bees and the scent of new flowers. Lissa was lost in her own thoughts, and when she looked up, Joe had stopped in front of a white cottage at the end of the street. She realized they had walked nearly to the edge of town. Beyond the house were cornfields and a few cattle lazily grazing, stopping occasionally to stare curiously at Lissa and Joe.

The house reminded her of her grandmother's, well taken care of and inviting. A white picket fence surrounded the neat front yard with its beds of roses and canna. A purple clematis vine, in full bloom, cascaded over the front-porch entrance, spilling its profusion of flowers like exploding fireworks. Joe started up the sidewalk, and Lissa hurried after him, wondering what he was doing. The windows had no curtains, and the house looked deserted.

"Want to go in?" he asked as he stopped at the foot of the porch steps.

Lissa frowned. "Do you know these people?"

"Not exactly. But I own the house."

She was still standing there staring after him as he unlocked the door. When she finally walked into the living room, Joe was standing in front of a small fireplace. Suzanne was babbling in pleasure, her wide eyes taking in everything about the room.

"They didn't use the fireplace the last several years," Joe said without turning around. "The house belonged to a retired couple who moved to Florida. I'll have to get someone out to check the chimney."

"It's a lovely house," Lissa said, taking Suzanne from him when the baby reached out her arms, and balancing her against her left shoulder. She walked slowly through the living room to the small dining room with its built-in mahogany cupboard and matching window seat. The window was large and overlooked a flower bed and what appeared to be an apple tree in the side yard.

Lissa continued wandering through the house, noticing the small details that indicated it had been a much-cherished home—the burnished wood floors and the braided rug that had been left behind, the pantry with a few jars of homemade jelly still sitting on the shelves and the glassed-in back porch that opened on to the spacious backyard that was filled with fruit trees, berry bushes and flower beds.

She was staring out the kitchen window, watching a robin in the willow tree when she felt Joe come to stand behind her. Suzanne, her head on Lissa's shoulder, laughed and held out a hand to him.

"There are three bedrooms upstairs and a full bath," he said. "One of the bedrooms looks out over the apple tree. It seemed perfect for Suzanne, especially since the tree's big enough for a swing."

"It has a lot of rooms," she said, thinking of the other bedrooms.

She turned around when he didn't say anything, and he shrugged. "I like houses with a lot of rooms. I suppose I always wanted a big family."

"More children?" she asked softly.

"At one time I did," he said, his eyes shuttered.

"But why did you buy such a...homey house if it was just for me?" she demanded. It wasn't the house a man would buy for his mistress.

Joe shrugged. "Did you know there's an old toy chest the previous owners left in what would have been Suzanne's bedroom? Their own daughter grew up there."

"I can't live here," she whispered, her voice ragged, her heart breaking. She loved the house; she loved Joe. But she couldn't accept his terms.

"Not even if I promise to stay away?" he said, his own voice sounding harsh and unnatural. "To let you live here alone?"

"No!" The baby turned at the sharpness in her mother's voice, her eyes wide and seeking reassurance. Lissa gently patted her, but her own gaze couldn't leave Joe's face. "I can't let you do this to me," she said. "I can't live in a house you bought for me, and I can't be your mistress."

"You're making it sound like a financial transaction," he said angrily.

"It is," she told him, trying to make him understand. "Someday I'd like a home of my own and more children. This is a wonderful house, but I'd grow to hate it—and myself—if I accepted your offer. It could never be a home under those conditions."

"But you like it?" he persisted.

"Of course I like it. It's—" She stopped short of admitting it was what she'd always dreamed of as a home. "It's lovely."

"I suppose I could rent it out," he said after a long pause. "It needs a little work." Then something else occurred to him. "Where are you going to go when Mrs. McGee opens her shop?"

Lissa had been wondering that, too. There weren't a lot of apartments in her rent range. "I'll think of something," she assured him.

"I don't want you and the baby in some dump," he said, his frown deepening. "I want to see the place before you sign any papers."

"I'm *not* giving you final approval on where I live," she informed him.

"We'll see."

She tried not to look back when they started down the sidewalk after Joe had locked the door. But it was hard. It was a beautiful house, and under different circumstances she would have jumped at the chance to live there. But not under Joe's conditions. She was paying a heavy price for her independence, but she would be damned if she'd let any man dictate her life, much less Joe Douglas.

Lissa worked a short shift at the store that evening and when Joe picked her up he was still crabby. When Lissa started to get the baby ready for bed, Joe tried to take over, insisting that she couldn't possibly do it herself. Irritated, she shoved his hands aside, only to discover that the baby wasn't going to have a bath if she didn't let Joe help.

He took over again with that arrogant male attitude of his, and Lissa gritted her teeth. Once Suzanne was in bed Lissa avoided Joe, even to the point of getting herself ready for bed without his help. She managed fairly well until she got to the underwear, and then she finally had to resort to tugging her bra off over her head. She was tired and more than a little irritable by the time she struggled into the same pink nightgown she'd worn the night before.

She closed the door to her bedroom and lay down in the dark, listening to him prowling her kitchen. It was at least two hours later when she heard him make his way to the couch. Knowing he was only one wall away didn't make it any easier for her to sleep, and she tossed and turned, trying to get comfortable.

She drifted off briefly and then woke up, unable to slide back into sleep. She finally tiptoed from bed and checked the baby. Suzanne was fast asleep, and Lissa envied her.

Restlessly she wandered out to the kitchen. She didn't hear a sound from the living room, and she assumed that Joe was asleep. The kitchen window was open a crack, and she could hear a whippoorwill calling eerily in the night. She eased out of the apartment to the landing and then out the door to the balcony, closing it quietly behind her.

The lounge chair was slightly damp from the summer humidity and glistening in the golden moonlight, and she brushed it off with her hand before sitting down and hugging her knees to her chest. She sat that way a long time, staring up at the stars and letting the night envelop her.

"Are you all right?"

She jumped at the sound of his voice, her head jerking around to find him standing in the doorway in his jeans. They were zipped, but in the glow from the moon she could see that they weren't snapped. He wore neither shoes nor shirt, and his bare skin was gilded in the moonlight. He looked like a statue of a god. He didn't move, and in the dark she couldn't see his face. But the tension in his body was evident.

"What are you doing out here?" he asked when she continued to stare at him.

"I couldn't sleep."

"Neither could I."

The night cloaked them, and Lissa rose from the lounge chair and went to stand by the railing, her back to Joe. She couldn't let herself stand too close to him; she hungered for him too much, and she knew that Joe was capable of wearing down her resolve. She'd sworn she wouldn't become his mistress, wouldn't let him dictate where she would live and pay her way, leaving her to wonder when he'd discard her. But it was so hard not to turn to his sheltering arms, to let him bring their bodies together until everything else in the world paled to insignificance.

"Why do you build things?" she asked quietly, and she knew it wasn't a question he was expecting. "What made you want to build bridges?"

She could feel him considering her question. "I had a talent for engineering," he said at last. "I was the one in the family who always wanted to put things together. Half the time that meant I had to take them apart first, and that drove my mother crazy."

Lissa smiled in the dark. "You'd better hire on as a consultant to Mrs. McGee before she opens her shop," she said. "Especially if she's going to be tearing apart small appliances. She'll electrocute half the town."

"I plan to give her a few lessons," he said significantly.

"That may not be enough to save lives," Lissa said dryly. She paused, then said, "But why did you go into construction?"

"I enjoyed it," he said simply. "To me, seeing a road grow where there was nothing or a bridge rise over a river is…satisfying. I built it, and I know that for years to come, people will use it, that it'll be a part of their lives."

Lissa nodded. She could understand that kind of satisfaction. "You built your company up yourself?"

"Yeah. It was rough going in the beginning, and I worked like the devil to make a go of it." Tension had crept into his voice, and she heard the strain. "Caroline tried to make me sell it and divide the profit with her during the divorce."

"Obviously she wasn't successful."

"She didn't even come close," Joe said, and in his tone Lissa felt the iron determination that he exercised when he chose. "No way anyone was taking the company from me." He fell silent again, then said, "What are you going to do when you get your degree?" She could hear that he'd moved closer.

"Teach. For the same reasons that you build things. It's useful, and hopefully I'll teach kids things they'll use the rest of their lives."

She would be a good teacher, he thought. She'd be the kind that kids came back to visit long after they'd left the school, maybe even bring kids of their own to meet her. There was something about her that reached out to people. She could touch a person even when they'd hidden themselves away in a cold and lonely place.

Lissa had made him ache for things he'd put aside years ago, a real home, kids, the sound of laughter. But wanting those things wasn't the same as being able to reach out for them. The closest he'd come so far was to try to get Lissa to share the house with him. She'd refused, out of her damn pride and independence, and he hadn't pushed her again. At one time he would have issued an ultimatum—either she shared the house with him or he'd get the hell out of her life altogether. But something inside him had changed in the short time he'd known Lissa. He wasn't willing to just walk away from her. Something was holding him here with her, and he could feel it binding him more tightly with each passing day. The funny thing was he wasn't chafing at the bindings.

She turned from the railing with the intention of going back to bed. It was late, and she had to work tomorrow. She stumbled slightly in the dark as her foot brushed the lounge chair, and Joe's arms reached out to steady her. Both froze at the contact, and Lissa's breathing turned shallow.

"It's late," he murmured and moved to let her go, but he didn't. She felt his fingers tighten fractionally on her arm. The moonlight brushed the hard edges of his features, making them harsher, but his eyes and voice were filled with want.

Lissa whispered his name, and the light breeze seemed to carry it away into the night.

Joe started to kiss her, then stopped, and then couldn't seem to help himself. His mouth took hers hungrily, greedily, as though he would never get enough. At one time his possessiveness might have rankled, but now Lissa matched him in passion and need. She needed Joe right now more than she needed air for her starved lungs.

When he raised his head at last, she took a deep, shuddering breath. His fingers skimmed the bare flesh of her arms, setting her on fire before they stroked over her collarbone and down to her breasts. Her nipples tightened and hardened immediately for him, and she groaned weakly as his thumbs wreaked havoc on any remaining shreds of her self-control. Her hands clutched his arms as she swayed, and Joe's mouth sought her throat. "You're so beautiful, sweetheart," he murmured against her skin. "I don't have any control when I touch you."

"Neither do I," she admitted shakily.

She felt his warm breath fan her neck before he brought his head up. "It's late," he said for the second time, his voice laced with regret and need. "Go back inside." He put her away from him gently, his fingers lingering, and Lissa went back to her bedroom.

But she couldn't sleep. Her body was still on fire from Joe's touch, and her heart ached for the man she loved.

Nine

Lissa should have felt a sense of relief. Finals were over, and she received *A*s in both courses. Her work schedule was a little less taxing now that two college kids home for the summer were working part-time at the convenience store.

But it was two weeks since the night Joe had held her on the balcony, and he'd studiously avoided touching her since then.

He still insisted on cooking for her every day and helping with the baby, but he was careful not to touch her and it was driving her crazy. It felt like a standoff. She wouldn't share his house and he wouldn't share any intimacy. And from the brooding look that perpetually lined Joe's face, she wasn't sure which of them was suffering more.

Jay had already dashed across the hall to his own apartment to watch a favorite TV show that Saturday night as Joe finished washing the dinner dishes. "I'm taking Jay to

Pittman to a birthday party tomorrow," he said casually. "Want to ride along?"

Lissa put the clean plate she was holding into the cupboard and turned to study Joe's back. He looked tense, but then he'd been nothing else for two weeks.

"Sure," she said, wondering if she'd regret her acceptance. He hadn't been the best company, though she was certainly grateful to him for all the help he'd provided. She was as edgy as he was, and she had to shoulder at least part of the blame for the way they'd sniped at each other the past few days.

They were both tired, Lissa of trying to fight for her independence and Joe from trying not to touch her or to face his own vulnerability. Lissa knew that they were both clinging tenaciously to thin ropes from the past, to behaviors that had carried each through rough times. But it was a losing battle.

They left in the truck the next morning, Jay a physical and emotional buffer as he sat between Joe and Lissa. Mrs. McGee had volunteered to watch Suzanne and was planning to take her on a walk. Jay chattered most of the trip, and his cheerfulness was almost contagious.

"Show her the fishing hole!" Jay cried when they turned off the highway onto a county road, a shortcut to Pittman.

"Okay," Joe said, sparing a quick glance at Lissa. He pulled the truck over, and Lissa got out, Jay racing to get ahead of her and lead the way. "Down here!" he called, going through some trees at the side of the road.

Joe followed more slowly, and when Lissa turned around, his eyes were on her. "Should we be here?" she asked. "Doesn't the owner mind?"

"A friend of mine owns this land," Joe said. "It's part of his farm. Jay and I have gone fishing here since he was old enough to hold a pole."

Lissa slipped a bit on the mud as Jay led them down an embankment, and Joe reached out and held her good arm. She stopped and looked at him, seeing such intensity on his face that it nearly stole her breath. She turned away immediately, and Joe released her arm.

"Now this is where I caught that big bass," Jay said importantly as they came to a stop at the bottom of the embankment. Sunlight danced on the river, as though some giant hand had tossed diamonds over it. Trees leaned out from the bank, their roots clutching the ground like gnarled fingers. Frogs sang from their hiding places, and Lissa spotted a turtle sunning itself on a log.

"How big was it?" Lissa asked Jay, figuring this was the question fishermen had loved since time immemorial.

Jay grinned and held out his hands two feet apart. Joe cleared his throat, his eyebrows rising, and Jay's hands moved in fractionally. "It was a whopper," Jay said. "Dad and me cleaned it and fried it right here."

"Best fish I ever ate," Joe confirmed. His eyes were fond and proud as he watched his son.

"Why don't we come fishing tomorrow?" Jay said, enthused over his sudden idea. "We could bring Lissa. You like to fish, don't you, Lissa?"

"It's been years," she said, trying to give Joe a way out.

"Now, Son—" Joe began, stopping when he saw the disappointment in Jay's face. "Not tomorrow," he said, glancing at Lissa. "I have work to do. But maybe next weekend."

Jay ran off to check the tree around the bend where he'd spied a squirrel nest the last time he was here. Joe was standing by the water, staring down at his reflection with his hands jammed in his pockets.

"Jay's the only person I've ever brought here," he said without looking at her. "Caroline had no interest in fishing."

"I can't say I'm a gung-ho fisherman," she told him.
"But I would like to come fishing sometime with you and
Jay."

"You don't have to," he told her as he bent to pluck a
stem of grass and worry it between his thumb and finger. "It
was only an idea."

"Why would you think I wouldn't want to come?" she
said, frowning down at him.

"Because you have an aversion to anything I want you to
do," he said roughly. He stood and faced her, his jaw a tight
line.

Lissa sighed. She supposed it must seem that way to him.
"It's not that I'm opposed to anything you suggest," she
told him. "It's just that you don't *suggest* most of the time.
You *order*."

"Me? Order you around?" He sounded incredulous, and
Lissa planted her one hand on one hip.

"Order," Lissa confirmed. "You have this terrible bossy
streak. We'd do much better if you'd make suggestions instead of just telling me what to do."

"And you have this terrible stubborn streak," he countered.

"Well, there you have it," she said airily.

A smile played around the corners of Joe's mouth.
"Could I make a suggestion?"

"What is it?" she asked suspiciously.

"That you kiss me," he said. "It's not an order. More like
a request."

Lissa felt herself warming. "I think I can manage that."

Joe cupped her chin in one hand and tilted up her face.
Slowly his mouth came down on hers, brushing her lips
lightly, then with more insistence. Lissa responded immediately, her lips parting for his, her arm winding around his
neck.

"Hey, you guys!" Jay called. "Come see the squirrels!"

Joe sighed and put Lissa gently away from him. "Come on," he said. "No rest for the wicked."

An hour later, they dropped Jay at his party, and Joe gave him last-minute instructions about saying please and thank you. He told Jay they'd be back to pick him up in three hours.

Joe drove around town, and it surprised Lissa that she'd forgotten so much about the place since she'd lived there. It was like seeing it through different eyes, being with Joe.

"This," he informed her with a grin as he turned the truck onto a wide, straight road that led out of town, "is where all the hell-raising teenage boys raced their cars on Saturday nights."

"Not you, of course," she said with mocking insincerity.

His grin broadened, and he pulled the truck to the curb. "I had this incredible little Mustang. I bought it with money from a part-time job, and I rebuilt the engine myself."

"And you beat all the young comers in their souped-up jalopies," she said, looking down the street and having no trouble imagining him as a hell-raising teenager.

"Aw, you guessed."

Lissa laughed. "I bet that for your whole life you've impressed every female who's ever laid eyes on you," she said.

"There was one who was immune," he said, and the self-mockery in his tone made her look at him. He was watching her with glittering, unfathomable eyes.

"Oh?"

"She thought I was too bossy," he said, shrugging. "She doesn't need anyone or anything, least of all from me."

"That's where you're wrong," she informed him.

Now it was his turn. "Oh?"

"Yeah. She needs a little emotional support, a little tenderness, a little..." She almost said *love,* but she didn't.

"And what does she think the last couple of weeks have been about?" he demanded, more than a little indignant and maybe even a little hurt, if she read him right.

"Joe," she said gently, her hand sliding over to touch his. "I want more than your talents and your time."

He looked down at her hand, his brows knitting.

"And your incredible good looks," she teased him, trying to keep the tone light because she wanted to cry.

"Lissa," he said quietly, dark eyes probing hers, "I'm doing the best I can."

"And your best is pretty wonderful," she told him. "My God, a man who cooks like you do, loves kids and takes care of me like I'm his grandmother's fine china—well, I guess you know you're every woman's dream of winning the relationship lottery."

He gave her a game smile. "You know how I love it when you give me the business." His fingers tightened on hers, and he sobered. "It's not enough for you, is it, Lissa?"

Her own smile faltered. "I've lived on other people's terms most of my life, Joe. I don't want to do that again. I don't want to give myself—and my life—up to someone else."

He knew what strength she had to call forth to tell him that. He could see the struggle and the sadness in her face, that beautiful, expressive face that had haunted him from the first day he saw her. That was what he'd admired about Lissa, her forthrightness whatever the personal cost.

They sat with their fingers entwined, their eyes focused somewhere outside the truck, as if it hurt too much to look at each other.

"What happened to your car?" she asked at last, her voice little more than a whisper. "The Mustang that ruled the streets."

He didn't answer for a long minute, until she thought he wouldn't answer at all. And when he did, it wasn't what she expected.

"It's in some junkyard now, or pieces of it anyway." The fingers on her hand curled around to her palm and stroked. "My brother wrecked it. I'd just beaten some little Chevy from across town, and I was feeling like big stuff. One of the cheerleaders was hanging all over me. We were at the local hamburger shack." He paused, letting his eyes graze her face, taking in the stark vulnerability. "So my brother took the keys I'd left in my jacket pocket and drove off. He lost it on a curve at the bluffs. He didn't get hurt . . . he jumped out of the car in time . . . but my Mustang went into a ravine. End of my racing career." He expelled his breath tightly, as though his chest was constricted. "He had to ruin what he couldn't have. It's been years since I even thought about that car."

"Joe, I'm sorry," she said.

Lissa ached for him, but she felt as though they'd crossed some invisible barrier. She suspected he hadn't faced that particular truth with anyone else before and she treasured his honesty.

It surprised Joe that he'd come this far. He could face the painful truth with no rancor. He'd made his peace with his memories, and he had a brother again—one who had foibles, a man who had hurt people, but who had also had a capacity for good. He could remember the wrecked car, but he could also remember his brother pointing out the constellations to Jay.

"What do you say I show you my house?" he suggested, the smile back on his face, though it wasn't jaunty. "I was hoping I could take you to meet Mom, but she's out of town on vacation. She signs up for all those group tours and goes trekking around the country on a bus. We'll catch her next trip."

Lissa felt a knot in her throat. It shouldn't have surprised her that Joe would want her to meet his mother. But somehow she hadn't foreseen it. And that made her realize that some small part of her still expected the worst from Joe.

"What are you thinking about?" he asked quietly after stealing a look at her face. He'd pulled the truck back onto the street and was heading across town.

"That I haven't appreciated you enough," she said, smiling at him.

Joe's brows went up. "Yeah? Well, maybe we can find some way you can appreciate me more." He grinned crookedly. "Some small way."

"Right." She found herself grinning back at him.

The house was on a shady street, a small brick home not unlike the others surrounding it. The big oaks in the front cast it in cool shadows during the hot part of the day, making the interior that much more of a surprise to Lissa when she entered.

"I knocked out a wall and did a little fixing up," Joe said modestly as Lissa looked around in admiration. A little fixing up was an understatement. The bright, airy kitchen was open to the living room, and both blended into the sunroom that was three steps lower and adjoining the other two. Warm oak cabinets and a skylight complimented the pale yellow tile in the kitchen. The living room and sunroom were furnished with more oak and cherry and some colorful pillows.

"This is beautiful," Lissa said.

"I picked out the furniture at little antique shops when I was on jobs," he told her, putting his hand at the small of her back and propelling her down the hallway from the living room. "I enlarged the bathroom."

"Enlarged?" she echoed wanly when she saw it.

It was something out of those glossy magazines she always leafed through at the dentist's office. The walls were mirrored, the floor tiled in a subtle blue, and a skylight sent warm shafts of sun filtering through the room. The room was divided in half by a wall of frosted glass blocks, and when she stepped to the archway, she saw both a sunken tub and hot tub nestled in a nook surrounded by tiled steps and beyond that blue carpeting. Tall, green plants stood in two of the corners, making the whole room look like a tropical paradise. Thick blue bath towels were piled by the steps.

"The work gave me something to do in my free time," he said, anticipating her question. "I'd planned to sell the house, but Jay liked it, and I did, too." He shrugged. "I know it's not your usual sort of bachelor digs."

"No," she breathed. "It certainly isn't."

"The bedroom's through here," he said, pointing to a door.

She walked through and stopped just inside the door. Like the rest of the house, the room was spacious and light. A four-poster oak bed with a white comforter was against one wall, beside it an oak nightstand. The bare wood floors were covered with colorful braided rugs, and in one corner was a basket of dried flowers. A white pitcher and bowl with blue flowers sat on top of an antique dresser with a towel bar.

The windows were large, the curtains a deep blue that looked striking against the eggshell-colored walls. Outside she could see a grapevine and evergreens.

"Do you like it?" he asked from behind her.

"You have excellent taste," she said dryly, shaking her head. "It's gorgeous."

But he didn't answer. Lissa could feel him standing behind her, could feel his eyes on her. Slowly she turned and met his turbulent gaze.

"Joe," she murmured.

"This is killing me, Lissa," he said. His hand reached out, stopped hesitantly, then gently cupped her cheek. "I want you so bad."

She took a deep, shaky breath. "Joe—" It was all she said. Her eyes said the rest. She needed him so much. She needed his strength and his caring. She needed this man more than she'd needed anyone in her life.

Without a word Joe picked her up and carried her to the bed, laying her down and letting her look into his eyes and see the raw need. No woman had ever affected him like this. He was hungry for her all the time. When he touched her, a fire raged inside his belly.

He lay beside her, pressing a hard kiss on her mouth as his hands framed her face. Neither spoke; they were beyond words, and they rushed to undress each other. In their haste their clothes ended up in a mingled heap on the floor. She was slowed by her cast, and Joe helped her, trying not to tear her red blouse and skirt. His hands were shaking by the time he got to her underwear. When she was naked, he knelt beside her and ran a hand down the length of her making her quiver beneath his touch. She whispered his name and held out her arms, but he shook his head.

"In a minute, baby," he murmured.

She wasn't surprised that he kept protection in the nightstand, and she was glad that he was taking the precautions for both of them. His lips followed his finger. "Let me make love to you, baby."

"Yes," she whispered, reaching for him.

He took care with her, but it was obvious he needed her badly. He propped a pillow under her hips, then knelt in front of her and hesitated. There was a haunted hunger in his eyes, and Lissa reached for him. "What is it, Joe?" she murmured.

"I don't want to hurt your arm," he said.

"It's all right. I think everything else will hurt a lot more if you don't make love to me now." She was desperate and a little scared of the need that was building inside her, but she tried to smile.

Joe searched her eyes and then slowly and deliberately he raised her legs and entered her. The pleasure, begun without preliminaries, was immediate and intense, making her moan. Joe leaned down to kiss and suck her nipples, and she grasped his hair, trying to hold him to her.

"You're so beautiful," he whispered urgently, his body movements bringing her such pleasure that she twisted beneath him. "I never wanted another woman to have any kind of hold on me again." He took a shuddering breath and moved again, making her arch with the sensations. "But with you..." he groaned.

"Do I have a hold on you?" she whispered, wanting some claim on him, something that made him even a little bit hers.

"Yes," he whispered hoarsely. "Yes. I can't stop wanting you. I can't get enough of you." As if to underscore his admission, he urged her on with his body, bringing her swiftly to the brink.

"Joe!" she cried out as the pleasure of his lovemaking overwhelmed her. "Joe...I...love you."

She felt his body shudder with release, and she couldn't be sure he'd even heard her words. Slowly her breathing returned to normal, and she dared a look at his face. He still held himself inside her, and he was watching her. Gently he leaned forward and brushed his mouth over hers. "It's going to be all right," he promised her, but he wasn't smiling.

She slept and wakened later when he gently brushed the hair from her face.

"Is this house any more acceptable to you than the other one?" he asked abruptly.

"What?" she murmured, not understanding.

"This house. Do you like it?"

"What are you saying?"

"I'm asking if you'd live here with me."

The words refused to sink in, and she turned in his arms and stared at him. His face was tight and his dark eyes had turned into night.

"Joe?" she whispered shakily.

"It's no one-day-I'm-here-and-the-next-I'm-not arrangement," he assured her, raising up on his elbow. "This is *my* house, Lissa, not a house I bought just to lure you into. I'm asking you to share it with me."

She looked back at him, wanting to believe in him, in their future, clinging to hope.

"I'm scared," she whispered.

"So am I, honey," he murmured, smiling as he kissed her gently. "So am I." He gathered her into his arms. "But I'm here with you. I won't leave you. Let me show you."

His hands moved over her, arousing her to straining desire in seconds. Lissa groaned and clutched him to her. There was no slow climb to passion with her and Joe. Emotions sparked between them like kindling in an inferno. As Lissa gave herself over to the devouring passion, her mind and body spun out of her control and she clung to Joe, crying out his name. She gave him everything, heart and soul, and she told him in her throaty whispers. And when they had both gone up in flames, their rapture shattering the tension, they found solace in each other's arms. Joe held her with aching tenderness, and Lissa caressed his hard chest, feeling the pounding cadence of his heart.

The silence stretched around them and became peace.

"It's time to go," he whispered at last, hovering above her and teasing her with light kisses. "At least I think it's time to go. I no longer own a reliable timepiece."

Lissa smiled and reached up to pull him down again for a proper kiss, and then he helped her dress.

"Joe?" she asked softly as he was pulling on his shoes after dressing her.

"What is it, honey?" He stood and stroked her hair. He couldn't seem to touch her enough.

"The house, Joe. How can I live here and still work and go to school?"

He sat down again on the edge of the bed. "Damned if I know," he groaned. "Lissa—" He broke off and let himself fall back on the bed, his eyes closing, his arms at shoulder level, as if he was about to make one of those snow angels that Lissa used to make as a kid. He groaned again and opened his eyes to look at her. "You could move into the other house?" he suggested hopefully.

"I don't know, Joe," she said helplessly. She wanted to— God knew she wanted to be close to him. But at what price? "It's not that I don't want to," she told him, trying to make him understand. "It's just that I need more from you. I need to know that you'll be there, not every day maybe, but at least as much as you can. I need...commitment. Joe, I love you."

There, she'd said it. It was what she'd wanted all her life from every person she'd cared about. And she'd received it only from her grandmother. And that, she felt, was only a grudging commitment; her grandmother had already raised her own child and had taken in Lissa out of responsibility. No one else had been there for her before, and for the first time in her life she was asking for that. She knew that Joe was always there for her, he'd shown her in every conceivable way...except words. She needed the words.

Lissa had never asked for anything for herself before, certainly not from a man, and the pulse at her temple throbbed unsteadily. She felt more naked than she had in his arms.

Joe sat up slowly, his eyes grazing her face as gently as his hand had done before. He knew how vulnerable she was. He knew how much of the real Lissa he was seeing, how much she was letting him see. Her eyes were wide and blue and trusting. She was asking for something so simple, just for him to tell her he'd be there for her.

He'd do anything in his power for her, but he wasn't going to make a promise he might not keep. All he knew was that he'd do the best he could.

"Joe," she said again, softly, and his eyes focused on the woman before him, the woman who had such power over him.

Joe stood and pulled her into his arms. "Look at me, baby," he whispered. "You know all about me, don't you? It's like I told you before—I do what I have to do. And what I have to do is take care of you. I can't promise any more or any less. But I know one thing. I'm in love with you." His hands caressed her, his eyes sought out the shadows in her own.

Her breath left her in a soft whoosh, and she let herself lean against him. "What do we do now?" she whispered against his chest.

He tilted her chin up and gave her a gentle smile. "We go pick up my son, and then we drive home and figure out what the hell we're going to do about these two damn houses I own."

Ten

They postponed any talk about housing after they got back that day, because Jay had eaten too much ice cream and cake, and he spent the evening propped on Lissa's couch drinking 7-Up and moaning.

"It was a great party, Dad," he said between moans and sips. "And I *danced.*"

"Did you now, son?"

"Yeah. And I wasn't too bad." Jay grinned, then immediately took a sip of soda. "You and Lissa were great teachers."

"Glad to hear it," Joe said, his eyes seeking out Lissa's as she came into the living room with Suzanne. "We've just been given a compliment," Joe told her. "Seems we're pretty good dancing teachers. We just might get a chance to polish our fancy footwork, too."

"What do you mean?" She handed Suzanne to Joe, then sat down in the rocking chair he'd patched for her. Her eyes were on him now, questioning.

"It looks like my company will be doing a road project in the southern part of the state in a year or so. I got the call after we got back." He reached over from the couch and let his fingers trail along her wrist. "I used to go down that way in the summer for vacation. There are some clubs there with terrific bands. And great fishing, too," he added, ruffling Jay's hair.

"Sounds nice," Lissa said, but she couldn't summon up the enthusiasm she should feel for the new job. Joe looked at her, and she turned her attention to the baby.

She slipped out of the living room as Joe was taking Jay back to his own bed in the other apartment. She put Suzanne down for the night and stood looking down at her daughter who was murmuring sleepily to herself. The door opened and closed softly, and she heard Joe come up behind her. When she turned around in the dark, he was standing so close that her arm brushed his. "What's wrong, Lissa?" he demanded softly.

She glanced back at her baby, sleeping now, and walked past Joe to the kitchen. He followed, stopping when she did and putting a tentative hand on her shoulder. "Come on, baby," he coaxed her. "Tell me about it."

She turned around then, but took a step backward so that his hand fell away. "The new job," she said, shrugging. "You'll be gone."

Joe frowned. "I'll always be leaving for one job or another. I thought you understood that."

"I suppose in theory I did," she admitted. "But all this talk of houses made me think, well, that we'd be together."

"We will," he told her, his hands coming to rest on his hips. "But I can't give up my work, Lissa."

"I know." She turned away from him.

"It's going to be all right," he said from behind her. "Believe me, baby."

The phone rang in his apartment, and he started for the door after a long, hard look at Lissa. Jay met him in the hall. "It's for you, Dad. It's Mr. Cassidy. He says it's about some papers you were filing."

Joe looked back sharply at Lissa as if he wanted to say something else, but she was already closing the door.

She got herself ready for bed without his help and then paced the bedroom, tired but strangely restless. Joe had said he'd try to be there for her, but it wasn't going to happen. There would always be the next job and then the one after that. He'd be in her life when it was convenient, and when it wasn't he'd be gone. She sank down on the bed, the sadness and loss sinking in.

Cassidy. Why was that name familiar? It nudged her subconscious like a persistent insect as she turned back the bed covers and set her alarm clock. It tickled the edges of memory as she slid between the sheets and tried to settle into a comfortable position.

She was just drifting off to sleep when it came to her. *Cassidy!* The high-powered lawyer who'd gotten custody of Jay for Joe! The man who specialized in custody cases.

Joe wouldn't, she told herself as she sat bolt upright in bed. He *couldn't* do that to her. She trusted him and he knew it. But he'd told her himself that he would do what he had to do, and she believed him.

He was already planning his life after her, planning the next job that would take him away. That would mean he wouldn't be close enough to spend time with Suzanne, and Joe Douglas was going to remedy that. He'd made it plain that he wanted certain standards met where the baby was concerned, and if she couldn't meet those standards, then he'd take care of it. He'd get what he wanted one way or the other. If she wouldn't move into his house, he'd make sure he had the baby anyway.

He was taking care of it all right. Dear God, she was in love with the man, and he was going to try to take her child.

Maybe she'd been wrong, and he'd never felt anything for her. He couldn't, not with what he was doing now.

She lay awake the rest of the night, staring at the ceiling, crying so hard that the tears ran into her hair and ears, and wondering where she could go that Joe wouldn't find her.

"How could you?" she whispered fiercely in the dark. "How could you when I love you so much?"

She locked the door and didn't answer his knock the next morning. After she heard him leave with Jay, she called Mrs. McGee to help her pack a few things for herself and Suzanne, and with her landlady's assistance, loaded up her car.

She'd rebuilt her life once, and she could do it again, no matter how much she was hurting inside. She wanted everything from Joe. She'd gambled that he could give it to her... and she'd lost.

"I'll be gone for a while," she told Mrs. McGee as she gave her the key. "I'm going to visit a friend. I'm not sure how long I'll be gone, but I'll let you know."

Lissa didn't even know where she was going, but she hoped she was convincing enough for Mrs. McGee. She left her standing on her porch, looking puzzled.

The next stop was the convenience store.

Her car died twice on the way, but she managed to restart it each time. Bonnie Ann was behind the counter when she walked in the door.

"I have to go away for awhile," Lissa said without preamble. "I'm not scheduled to work until tomorrow night, but can you get the new kids to fill in for me?"

"You're going away?" Bonnie Ann repeated with a frown. "Where? Why?"

"I can't explain now. And I don't know how long I'll be gone."

"But, Lissa—"

"I can't explain now, Bonnie Ann. I'll call you later."

Lissa started for the door just as Joe's truck pulled into the parking lot. She nearly panicked, knowing she couldn't make it to the car without him seeing her. But she had no choice. Tightening her grip on Suzanne who was waving over her shoulder to Bonnie Ann, Lissa firmly pushed open the door and strode toward her car.

"Lissa!" he called, and when she didn't stop or look back at him, he broke into a jog. He caught up with her just as she reached for the door handle.

"What the hell are you doing?" he demanded, his hand closing over her wrist.

"Let go of me!" she cried, trying to jerk free.

"Lissa! What's gotten into you? Where have you been? I've been looking all over for you." His other hand tried to turn her face toward him, but she wouldn't let him. It was a useless struggle, and she knew it was over before it had barely begun. Stubborn, proud and defiant, she finally stood still, her back against the car door. Suzanne began to fuss, and Lissa patted her gently without looking at Joe.

"Baby, what's the matter?" he demanded, his voice as determined but more gentle. "What's happened?"

She let herself look at him then, and her heart broke in two just as she'd known it would. She couldn't forgive him for what he was doing to her, but she still loved him. She'd always love him.

"You can't take Suzanne!" she said, but it was more a plea than a statement.

"Take Suzanne? What are you talking about?" His hand reached out for her again, but he stopped when he saw the expression in her eyes. "Lissa?" He did touch her then, stroking back her hair, his thumb laying a soft caress on her cheekbone.

"I know who Cassidy is," she told him, trying to hold the tears at bay. "I know what you're doing."

He still didn't seem to understand.

"I know he's the lawyer who got custody of Jay for you. But I can't let you have Suzanne, Joe. I don't care how much it will cost me, but I can't let you do it."

Comprehension began to dawn in his face, and his eyes grew thunderous. "You thought—" he exploded, stopping short. "How could you think I'd try to take your child?" he demanded, his hand on her wrist tightening. Then he read the anxiety on her face, and the tension seemed to drain out of him. "God in heaven, of course you'd think that," he muttered, his hand releasing her and raking through his hair. "I told you that enough times, didn't I? I threatened and bullied and cajoled, and I told you I'd do whatever I had to do. And I never once thought that you'd actually believe me." He shook his head, and she saw the vestige of anxiety in his eyes.

Something heavy was lifting from her heart. "You mean you wouldn't . . . ?" She closed her eyes in relief.

Quickly he shook his head. "Never, baby. I couldn't hurt you like that. I'd sooner cut out my own heart. Look at me, Lissa."

She was almost afraid of what she'd see in his face, but she let herself look into his eyes. What she saw there made her knees tremble.

"Cassidy's doing some other business for me," he told her gently. "He's putting the house here in your name."

"What? But why?"

Joe sighed and made a helpless gesture. "Because I'll do whatever it takes to convince you I'm in your life for the long haul. I'll always have jobs somewhere else. That never changes. But I'll take you and the baby with me whenever I can. And when I can't, I'll come home so often you'll get sick of seeing me."

"No," she whispered, shaking her head in wonderment. "I could never get tired of you."

"Lissa, you're so independent and strong. You're the one who talked about commitment, but I couldn't make myself believe that you needed me the way I need you. I knew I was falling in love with you the first moment I saw you in the store, but I couldn't let myself in for that kind of punishment again. So, I fought it every step of the way." His hands were trembling as they framed her face. "I've never needed anyone the way I need you, baby. I want to spend the rest of my life with you. I want to wake up with you every morning and have children with you and grow old with you."

She saw everything she'd ever wanted there in his eyes. All the love and all the cherishing a woman would ever need. He'd always been there for her, and she hadn't seen it, because she was afraid. He'd taken care of her and the baby because he needed to take care of her, but she'd seen only a man who was trying to run her life. She'd been too blind to see a man in love.

"I'm sorry," she whispered, reaching up to cover his hand with hers. "I was afraid you didn't want me, and I made myself believe the worst."

"There's nothing to be sorry about," he told her gently. "Not any more." Slowly he began to smile. "You don't know what time it is, do you?"

"Me?" she said shakily. "Not a clue. Why?"

"Because we're going to have to hide a working clock from Mrs. McGee if we're ever going to make appointments on time."

"Appointments?" she repeated in a daze.

"Yeah, appointments. For a blood test and a marriage license and a church. You *will* live with me after I marry you, won't you?" He looked a little worried, just enough to make her smile.

"Oh, yes," she assured him. "Definitely."

Bonnie Ann and her coterie of customers watched from
the doorway as Joe gathered Lissa in his arms, his mouth
seeking hers with a hunger that conveyed all his love. From
over his shoulder, Suzanne waved merrily at their audi-
ence.

Epilogue

He couldn't believe he'd come this far in his life. To want to get married again was nothing short of a miracle to Joe. And he did want to get married, though wearing a tux was something of a trial. That and the usual wedding jitters. He parked the truck in the church lot and shook his head ruefully as he got out.

He'd bet anything that Jay and Mrs. McGee were responsible for the streamers and tin cans that bounced from the back bumper. Everyone had stared when he'd driven down the street, most of them waving in amusement.

But today he didn't care. It was a brisk September day, and even though the sky was clouding up, he was marrying the woman he loved.

Lissa was sitting on the top step of the church when he came around the corner, and seeing her so pretty in a long, soft pink silk dress, flowers in her hair, made him smile through his nervousness. "Have I ever told you how beautiful you are?'' he asked, sitting beside her. "What are you doing out here anyway? Shouldn't you be inside putting a penny in your shoe or something?''

"I imagine so," she said agreeably. "Do you think we're early or late for the wedding?"

Joe glanced up at the sky. "I'd say it's close to noon. That would make us early."

"Did Mrs. McGee get her hands on your new calendar watch?" she asked in sympathy.

Joe nodded and glanced at the watch. "It says it's midnight Christmas Eve."

Lissa laughed. "It does sort of feel like Christmas, doesn't it? I mean the anticipation."

"Yeah, it does," he said, putting his arm around her shoulder and gently rubbing it. She'd had the cast off for a while now, but occasionally she got a twinge, and he wanted today to be perfect for her.

"I wonder why the minister isn't here yet," Lissa said, leaning into Joe's touch.

"I have a feeling he took his watch to Mrs. McGee's new shop, and so did the organist and everyone else in town," Joe said ruefully. "For some reason, her shop is a roaring success. Even though no one in town knows what time it really is, and toasters from here to the river are slinging bread at the ceiling. It's like living in the *Twilight Zone.*"

"It is," Lissa agreed, smiling. "But I kind of like it."

Joe wasn't sure that he'd admit he'd changed *that* much, to the point that he actually enjoyed Mrs. McGee's good-natured but misplaced efforts, but he was definitely more mellow about things in general.

He'd finished the work on Mrs. McGee's house, and her new shop had opened right on schedule. Now Mrs. McGee and her sister lived upstairs, and Joe and Lissa and Jay had moved into the little house across town.

A car pulled up in front of the church, and Joe and Lissa watched as the minister hopped out, the organist right behind him. "Good gracious!" he exclaimed. "Am I late? My watch must have stopped." Joe gave Lissa a look, and she tried not to laugh.

"I can't understand it!" the organist wailed. "I just had my kitchen clock fixed, and now it's running slow." She paused on the top step to straighten her skirt, smiling when she looked down at Joe and Lissa. "You make such a lovely couple," she said.

Right on their heels came Bonnie Ann, running as though she'd just spotted the finish line of a marathon. She screeched to a halt in front of them, holding up her long dress with one hand and anchoring her hat with the other.

"I finished the cake!" she announced. "You should see the bride and groom on the top layer. I made them out of marzipan. They look just like you. Oh! I've got your bouquet in the car! Wait until you see it, Lissa! Orchids! Did you know I grow orchids in my spare time?"

"Bonnie Ann, I wouldn't be surprised if you ran a Third World country in your spare time," Lissa assured her as Bonnie Ann raced back down the steps toward her car.

The next to arrive was Jay with Suzanne. Suzanne insisted on showing off her newfound balancing skills, and Jay held her hands while she pranced in place on the step and sang out in her own multi-syllable language.

"Where's Mrs. McGee?" Joe asked his son. "Did she drop you off and get lost?"

"Naw," Jay said. "She said she had to get your present out of the trunk."

"Ten to one it's a rebuilt toaster," Joe said, nudging Lissa.

"We'll be scraping English muffins off the ceiling," she agreed, laughing.

"Did you see how I decorated the truck?" Jay asked his dad, and Joe nodded.

"It was a fine job, son. Where'd you get all those cans?"

"Mrs. McGee's teaching me to cook, Dad. That way I can help out when you're working and Lissa's in class."

"Here comes trouble," Joe murmured under his breath as Mrs. McGee hurried up the walk carrying a large box.

"I found the perfect present for you!" she exclaimed, beaming widely.

"You didn't have to get us anything," Lissa told her, but Mrs. McGee would have none of that. "Oh, no, dear. Every wedding I've attended, I've given the bride and groom the same present. It's sort of a tradition. Gets them off on the right foot, you see." Still beaming, she headed inside with her box, calling over her shoulder, "It's an anniversary clock. I fine-tuned it myself."

Joe and Lissa managed to keep properly respectful, straight faces until she was inside, and then they both burst out laughing at the same time. "We'll never know when it's our fifth anniversary or our tenth," Lissa said, and this set them off again.

They were still laughing as other guests began arriving, and they stood side by side with Jay and the baby and shook hands, greeting friends who had come to wish them well. A few scattered raindrops fell, but not enough to dampen anyone's enthusiasm.

Joe's mother was among the last to arrive, stopping to smile and kiss them both before she went inside.

The organ music started and Jay picked up Suzanne. They were becoming a family, and they'd decided on a slightly unorthodox entrance with Jay and Suzanne walking with them down the aisle and standing with them during the ceremony. "You can still back out, maybe go elope somewhere," a grinning Jay told Lissa.

"No way," she informed him. "Bonnie Ann's gone to so much trouble, she'd pull a gun on all of us."

Joe offered Lissa his arm, and she took it, then stopped in her tracks, frowning. "That music," she said. "It's—it's from my Dinah Washington album."

Joe grinned and nodded. "'September in the Rain.' I gave it to the organist last night. She's a quick study."

It brought her memories of dancing with Joe in her kitchen, and it was perfect. She smiled up at him, loving him more than ever.

"Come on, Ms. Gray," Joe whispered just before he kissed her. "Time to go."

She kissed him back, putting all her love into it, and Jay started inside with Suzanne in his arms. Leaning over his shoulder, Suzanne blew them a kiss and hollered, "Boo-boo!"

* * * * *

SILHOUETTE® Desire®

MYSTERY MATES!

**Six sexy Bachelors explosively pair with
six sultry Bachelorettes to find the Valentine's
surprise of a lifetime.**

Get to know the mysterious men who breeze into the lives of these
unsuspecting women. Slowly uncover—as the heroines themselves
must do—the missing pieces of the puzzle that add up to hot, *hot*
heroes! You begin by knowing nothing about these enigmatic men,
but soon you'll know *everything....*

Heat up your winter with:

#763   THE COWBOY by Cait London

#764   THE STRANGER by Ryanne Corey

#765   THE RESCUER by Peggy Moreland

#766   THE WANDERER by Beverly Barton

#767   THE COP by Karen Leabo

#768   THE BACHELOR by Raye Morgan

Mystery Mates—coming in February from Silhouette Desire.
Because you never know who you'll meet....

SDMM

Take 4 bestselling love stories FREE

Plus get a FREE surprise gift!

**Silhouette Books
is proud to present
our best authors,
their best books...
and the best in
your reading pleasure!**

Throughout 1993, look for exciting books
by these top names in contemporary
romance:

CATHERINE COULTER—
Aftershocks in February

FERN MICHAELS—
Whisper My Name in March

DIANA PALMER—
Heather's Song in March

ELIZABETH LOWELL—
Love Song for a Raven in April

SANDRA BROWN
(previously published under
the pseudonym Erin St. Claire)—
Led Astray in April

LINDA HOWARD—
All That Glitters in May

When it comes to passion,
we wrote the book.

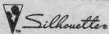

Silhouette®

BOBT1R

For all those readers who've been looking for something a little bit different, a little bit spooky, let Silhouette Books take you on a journey to the dark side of love with

SILHOUETTE *Shadows* ™

If you like your romance mixed with a hint of danger, a taste of something eerie and wild, you'll love Shadows. This new line will send a shiver down your spine and make your heart beat faster. It's full of romance and more—and some of your favorite authors will be featured right from the start. Look for our four launch titles wherever books are sold, because you won't want to miss a single one.

THE LAST CAVALIER—Heather Graham Pozzessere
WHO IS DEBORAH?—Elise Title
STRANGER IN THE MIST—Lee Karr
SWAMP SECRETS—Carla Cassidy

After that, look for two books every month, and prepare to tremble with fear—and passion.

SILHOUETTE SHADOWS, *coming your way in March.*

SHAD1